ASYLUM

ASYLUM

P.G. Wodehouse meets St. Paul

A Novel

TOM TRAVIS

For my dear wife, Anne

CONTENTS

INTRODUCTION

The original title for this opus minimus was *Paul and Plum – Joy Bringers*. The reason being that its two main protagonists, St Paul, and P.G. Wodehouse (a.k.a. Plum), had been for many years (after Jesus Christ, my family, and close friends) my biggest sources of joy in life. I became intrigued by the thought of what it might have been like (had it been possible) if the two of them had met. The idea would not go away. It percolated, or you might say, gestated, in my mind for years, until I really had to do something about it. I would, I decided, for my own satisfaction, create a scenario by which discourse could take place between these two giant purveyors of joy and, by so doing, be able to explore, in my imagination, what might have transpired.

It occurred to me that they did have something in common, other than their joy-bringing qualities, and that was that they had both spent time in captivity. Paul for disrupting Judaism, and in turn, the Roman Empire, by preaching about the

Messiah, Christ Jesus; and Plum for being an Englishman who happened to live in France when the Nazi hordes invaded in 1940. Well, there's a start, I thought, I could put them together in a prison cell and see what happens.

I seemed to spend an inordinate amount of time wrestling with the problem of the time difference and how someone who lived in the 20th century would be able to avoid complicating things by knowing and saying what was to happen in the future – and explaining that future to people who lived in the first century. Then, remembering Plum's ability to rub along with people in his unquestioning and kindly way, I realised that there was no one better suited to the task than Plum Wodehouse – that, along with me supporting him with a literary device to assist when doing so – provided the green light, as it were. And, so I began.

Being a habitual list maker, I decided to write down, in some order, the purpose – other than freeing my mind of the ever-recurring thoughts on the matter – for undertaking such an exercise. My list began, pretentiously, and in capital letters, PURPOSE OF BOOK – see I told you about the mental gestation process; my simple scenario had now developed into a book.

This is what I jotted down:

- To celebrate the lives of two good men.
- To display their better traits – concern for others, belief in the good in people.
- To contrast the two personalities – very different, but each kind and sympathetic.

- To take advantage of Plum's gentle humour, when combined with Paul's dour enthusiasm and drive.
- To write a story based in peace instead of death and violence (there is a conflict here, when considering the good derived from the violence in the story of Christ's crucifixion. But then his way, if followed, is one of peace and so that helps even things up).
- To show the positive aspects of mankind.
- To dispel cynicism.
- To build a spirit of optimism.
- To recognise dignity and respect.
- To explore the two protagonists and their motives.
- To amplify their attractive qualities for instruction and amusement.
- To reaffirm (as if that were necessary) the benefits to others of their having lived.
- To explore why the two of them are beacons of virtue to myself and so many others.

There you are, fourteen guidance points for my venture – three more than God gave to Moses for his. The notes continued for a couple more pages, with which I will not trouble you.

So, why change the title, *Joy Bringers* to that of *Asylum*? Well, for several reasons, really. When I started to plan my joyful assault, it occurred to me that the vicissitudes of life seem to conspire against unbridled joy making by sticking the oar in just when you think everything in the garden is blooming lovely. (Sorry about the mixed metaphors, but I'm sure you know what I mean). I must have been too optimistic...or, let's face it, naïve to think I could get my reader to buy into the idea that life is a bowl of small tree fruits of the genus *Prunus*. Here we have Paul and his pals being chased from pillar (and pillars were very popular with the Romans in those days and so there were plenty of them) to post by angry Sanhedrin and even more angry Roman soldiers, who banged them up in gaol at the drop of a Gladius. And then Plum Wodehouse steeped in the rigours of World War II, rounded up by the Nazis and interned in, what else but, a one–time asylum for the insane. Now, where's the joy in that?

It struck me that maybe the world in which we live is just one great big asylum for the insane. But then, with people like Paul and Plum having lived in it, there must be a brighter side. I first met Plum (by that I mean his work), when on a business trip from my home in Manchester to Leicester in about 1965. Standing on Leicester rail station platform, I was browsing one of those revolving bookstands when my eyes settled upon a book by P.G. Wodehouse. At the time I, was enjoying, thoroughly, the television series, *The World of Wooster* (the one that featured Ian Carmichael as Bertie Wooster and Dennis Price as his manservant Jeeves). Mmm I thought, as you do, I'll give this a go. I purchased said book and read it all the way home on the train. By the time we had pulled into Piccadilly Station, Manchester, I was hooked.

From then on, when stressed by the afore-mentioned, vicissitudes, I would escape by immersing myself in an adventure with Messrs Jeeves and Wooster or retire to a sunny spot within the walls of Blandings castle to be with the Honourable Galahad Threepwood, (or "Gally" to his friends, and I certainly counted myself as one). This was asylum of a different kind and by that, I mean the kind that my Oxford English Dictionary describes as: 'Shelter or protection from danger' – a precautionary measure that I took to prevent my asylum being described by those same editors of erudition at the OED as being: 'an institution for the care of people who are mentally ill.' Reading Wodehouse, during difficult times, proved to be the saviour of my sanity – a condition that must, I suspect, be a common occurrence amongst his many readers.

As far as my relationship with Paul, or as I must now call him, Saint Paul, I have, for several decades, been an occasional reader at my local church. I love the set of formularies that constitute the liturgy from which I read and enjoy them – not only as part of my religious instruction but also as *belles-lettres*. I fully appreciate not only the exquisite literature to be found in the Old Testament such as the Song of Solomon or the writings of Isaiah but, also, the beautiful New Testament letters of St Paul, (particularly Romans) which appear regularly on the lectern. What a towering intellect that man had – his organisational skills, his razor-sharp mind, and his gift as a writer of magnificent poetry and prose; all gain my attention and cause me to remain, as with Plum Wodehouse but in a different way, hooked.

So, off I set, in imagination, with my two joy-bringing heroes and what follows is my adventure…please join me, I hope you will…

Tom Travis, *April 2017*

CHAPTER ONE

The Letter

"Through here," said the prison guard, who had a distinct German accent and wore the uniform of the Nazi army, complete with the characteristic coalscuttle helmet. Plum entered a large area (he'd expected a smaller cell, similar to the one he had occupied at Loos Prison, in France. Plum, or to give him his full name, Pelham Grenville Wodehouse, an Englishman, had been living and working, peacefully with his wife, Ethel, as a writer of humorous novels, at Le Touquet on the Northern coast of France. After the Germans invaded France in 1940, they had tried on two occasions, to make their escape but had failed on both counts, due to their car breaking down. Plum was then officially interned by the occupying Germans and sent, initially, to a prison at Loos, a suburb of Lille; then by cattle truck, with forty others, to a Belgian Army barracks near Liege; he was then again moved to the Citadel at Huy before fetching up here at a converted asylum for the insane at Tost in

Upper Silesia (then in south-west Germany; now a part of Poland).

As the door slammed behind him, Plum observed that there were several people already in the cell. One, a small, swarthy man, approached him, hand outstretched. Plum was somewhat shocked and surprised that the man approaching was wearing a kind of dark green shift, a bright red cloak and leather sandals.

"Welcome," said the man. "My name is Saul, but my friends call me Paul. Welcome to our company of Good News, joy, hope and salvation."

That's a promising start, thought Plum; the goods that this chap is offering certainly hit the spot with me.

"Thank you. My name is Pelham but my friends call me Plum"

"Well then Plum, if I might call you that,"

"Please do", Replied Plum.

"Then let me introduce you to the others: This is Luke"… hands were shaken and smiles exchanged as Paul went on to introduce Aristarchus, Demas and Epaphras. "Oh," he exclaimed, "and I must not forget this small bundle of mischief, Onesimus."

What a startling coincidence, thought Plum, they all have the same names as characters in the new testament of the bible. He plumbed the depths of his memory of his years of church attendance to emerge with the further realisation that those very same people were all together in captivity with Saint Paul. This is extraordinary, he thought, before it dawned on him that someone, with whom he had been transported to this place, had told him that, before being converted to accommodate pris-oners, it used to be an asylum for the insane. That explains it, thought Plum; they have not yet finished the project and still have some of the previous inmates here. It is an obvious case of religious mania…they must think that they really are those biblical characters. Well, I had better make the most of the situation, it is no use making waves…the best thing when incarcerated is to survive by whatever means possible. I will just carry on as normal. Plum addressed the bright-eyed waif Onesimus:

And what do your friends call you?"

"Onesimus" replied the boy, a little crest-fallen.

"His name means, 'useful,'" said a smiling Paul.

"Mmm, useful? Then, that is what I will call you," said Plum.

"So," said a somewhat uplifted Onesimus, "when someone says to me, 'What do your friends call you? I'll be able to say, 'Useful.'"

Paul looked at this pleasant, congenial man, Plum, and thought, who is he, and why is he wearing those strange clothes? It was then that Plum noticed the quizzical expressions of Paul and his other cellmates – although they were trying not to be ill mannered – taking occasional glimpses at the way he, himself, was dressed. His grey Harris Tweed, three-piece suit, replete with plus-four trousers, from which protruded light grey, stocking-covered legs, neatly finished off at the base by thick, black, brogue shoe-covered feet, must, to them, have seemed somewhat bizarre. On consideration, Plum decided to avoid explanations in the hope that, eventually, both parties would become accustomed to their differences and carry on as normal.

Paul and his associates had often seen Roman legions returning from far-flung parts of the Empire, parading captives who were dressed in the ways of the people of their own lands. After all, the empire in which they lived covered an immense area and one was likely to be constantly surprised by seeing visitors from all parts of the world.

A space was made for Plum, where he could place his suitcase and typewriter case (another cause of great curiosity for his new friends).

"Where do I sleep?" enquired Plum.

"On the dog shelf," trilled Useful.

"The what?"

"The floor" said Paul, pointing to a space in the corner.

How wonderfully reminiscent of Loos Prison, thought Plum, remembering how, whilst there, he had had to sleep on a granite floor with only his clothes and Macintosh for bedding.

"Dare I ask what we might use as bedding?"

"You're wearing it," chirruped Useful.

More happy memories of Loos thought Plum… And that explains Paul's bright red cloak. That chap has obviously had previous experience of this kind of thing and comes equipped.

What Plum could not possibly know was that he really was in the company of the man who was to become Saint Paul, the human powerhouse who – through his realisation of the truth and meaning for the world of Christ's crucifixion and resurrection – laid the foundations on which the universal Christian church was to be built. Jesus may have appointed St Peter to be the rock on which his church would be erected but it fell to Paul to, unintendedly, draw up the plans for its construction. Also, unknown to Plum, the people who surrounded him in this dank, dark cell were really who they said they were.

What it was that brought Plum into contact with such

world-changing people, must remain only a matter for conjecture. According to Paul and Plums' followers, a lot of whom can now be found in both their camps, they were each bent on providing an entrée to paradise, whether, in Plums case, within the walls of his Eden-like fictional creation, Blandings Castle, here on earth, or, as Paul intended, in the next world. I suppose you might say that what they each had in common was that they were, without doubt, committed joy bringers.

◆

Weeks passed and Plum's relationship with his new friends strengthened. As he took a small break from the novel he was writing, Plum's eyes lifted from the typescript to refresh themselves by scanning his surroundings. He noticed that his, by now, dear friend Paul was sobbing quietly.

"What is this Paul? Are those tears on your cheeks?"

"My dear Plum," replied a very perturbed Paul, "I am in the middle of dictating to Luke, a letter to be sent to the members of the Church of God, at Corinth."

"And what is it that has made you so upset whilst doing so?"

"Well," said Paul, "On my last visit to the Corinthians I was appalled to discover that they are being diverted from the true teachings of Christ Jesus by a new group of missionaries of the Jesus movement. These 'sham apostles' are preaching the message that this godlike human, Jesus, enshrines superlative Jewish qualities and that he is the perfect model from which the whole world can be converted to Judaism and that Israel could then preside over a new order of justice and equity throughout the world."

"Is that a bad thing?"

"It certainly is, because they are espousing the power of our Lord Jesus, and the fact that He is a Jew, to advance their strategy of having all people convert to Judaism and to submit to its single law. They are employing earthly wisdom, philosophy and fine oratory to attain their elitist ends."

"Do you mean that they don't really believe in Jesus as the true Son of God?"

"They believe only," continued Paul, "that Jesus was a wise Jew who performed miracles and, like Moses and Elijah, was a perfect example of the tradition of Jewish wisdom. I doubt very much if they believe in the crucified Christ – in fact, they seem to have forgotten about that altogether – and they appear to have no appreciation of the power of the spirit."

"So," enquired Plum, "what are you saying to them in your letter?"

Paul explained:

"As the members of the Church of God at Corinth seem to be impressed by the boastful claims of these 'super apostles,' I now see that I have nothing to lose by doing a little boasting of my own, and that is what I mean to do. It is my intention to use humour to surprise them into realising the serious implications of their actions. I will compose a fool's speech."

"Ah, humour! That is my speciality," exclaimed Plum, eyes twinkling, "let me have a go at a little humorous boasting for you? I'll stop what I'm writing and get on with it immediately."

"My dear, dear Plum," answered Paul, "I do appreciate your kind concern and willingness to help, but I think that in this instance I can manage on my own."

"Oh, that is unfortunate," said a slightly dejected Plum, "humour is a serious business and requires the mind of a specialist"…but, brightening, added, "might I suggest that I wait until you've written your humorous bit of the admonishing missive, and then I can start giving it the old Wodehouse touch – retaining the feel of it, of course. The way I see it, you have nothing to lose… and may have something to gain."

"If it makes you happy, Plum, we'll try it your way. I'll give you sight of that particular part when the letter is finished."

"And very wise too," said a reassuring Plum.

Eventually, Paul, on finishing his 'Fool's Letter,' handed Plum a couple of pages. Plum sat upon his typewriter case, studied them for a while before placing his small brown leather suitcase on his knee, on top of which he balanced his typewriter and proceeded to hammer away on its keys. At length, Plum removed the sheet from the machine with a swift tug and announced, "What do you think of this?" and began to read:

"But if anyone wants some brazen speaking – I am still talking as a fool – then I can be as brazen as any of them, and about the same things. Brazen? Why, Jezebel and Delilah could have taken my correspondence course. Hebrews, are they? Then so am I. My dear old Jewish mother fed me so much chicken soup that, at mealtimes I had to wear a lifebelt.

Israelites? So am I. Why, my Israeli descendants go back so far that they knew the Dead Sea when it was only ill. Descendants of Abraham? So am I – In fact

21

my great, great, great grandfather was so pally with Abraham that he actually called him, 'Abe.'

The servants of Christ? I must be mad to say this, but so am I, and more than they: more because I have worked harder — I've worked my fingers to the elbows and I have been sent to prison so often, that my friends refer to me as' that gaolbird.' But, the prison authorities, because of my regular revisits to the old calaboose — which had now become my Alma Mater — not content with gaolbird, are species-specific in calling me a 'homing pigeon'. And, I might add, I've been whipped so many more times. Five times I had the thirty-nine lashes; three times I have been beaten with sticks; once I was stoned."

"Actually," chirruped Useful, getting into the swing, "he was stoned on every occasion – it was the only way he could stand the pain of the lashings,"

"Cheeky… but chuckle-worthy," said Plum.

"*Too* cheeky," said an irritated (but mildly amused) Paul.

Plum resumed his reading of the letter:

'Three times I have been shipwrecked, and once adrift in the open sea for a night and a day. In fact, my frail craft became a social centre for the neighbourhood sharks. "Let us all go around to Paul's boat," sharks had said to one another. "I'm told, if you don't mind waiting for a night and a day, the food is promising — and you had better remember to use

22

your table napkin, as It is likely to fall right into your lap.

Constantly travelling, I have been in danger from rivers and in danger from brigands, in danger from my own people and in danger from pagans; in danger in the towns, in danger in the open country, in danger at sea and in danger from so-called brothers. I consulted a specialist counsellor about it. "I'm pleased to tell you," he said "that you're not imagining all this impending danger. No," he reassured, handing me a slip on which was written the total of his fat fee, "it's the real McCoy alright. Yep, it is not your mind playing you tricks. That is twenty-four carat Danger with a capital 'D.'" After which, I kicked his couch and left, full to the brim of dudgeon.

I have worked and laboured, often without sleep; I have been hungry and thirsty and often starving; I have been in the cold without clothes."

"That last, 'Without clothes' bit," interjected Useful, "is a secret compulsion that he's struggling with but he's getting there, aren't you Paul?"

"Useful!" rebuked Paul, (who, by now, was calling him by the name that Plum had settled upon). "This time you've gone too far."

"Sorry Paul," replied Useful, "but it *was* Plum who started it."

"Well, what do you think?" enquired Plum of Paul.

"Do you really think Plum, that this will help change the minds of the church members at Corinth?"

"It's like money in the bank," Plum reassured him.

"Let me think about it," replied a bewildered Paul, still in shock.

◆

"Paul," said Plum, whilst taking a break from his writing, and needing an opening gambit with which to start a conversation, "when not contemplating the wonders of a prison wall and the beautiful, though robust, utterances written upon it by previous occupants, what do you do to earn your daily crust?"

"O, my work?" replied Paul, "I have a business that makes and supplies leather tents."

"Did you develop it yourself or is it a family concern?"

"It has been in the family for generations."

"Is it profitable?"

"Reasonably," replied Paul. "When I'm not writing to members of the various churches in the places I have visited to plant the seeds of Christianity, I am writing to clients and suppliers in an attempt to keep my business afloat."

"Why tents?"

"Although it was one of my great grandfathers who decided upon which area of business to enter, I should imagine he had observed a need for tents and decided to fulfil that need."

"Oh, I see," said Plum, It's the same for me. I used to read a magazine to see what the editor likes and submit a story to suit... Common sense, I suppose."

"Common sense?" queried Paul...what an interesting phrase!"

"I learned it, indirectly, from a man called Thomas Paine," said Plum.

"You'll have to tell me about Mr Paine sometime, he sounds intriguing."

"From what I know about you so far Paul, I doubt that you will agree with much that he had to say."

"We digress." said Paul, "Now, where were we? Oh yes, on starting a business...if you are in a particular area and decide to start a business, then the obvious thing to do would be to look around to see what is happening, and what people are needing, for instance. To put it simply, if you were setting up shop on the edge of an arid dessert you would not think, Mmm I think I will sell rainwear – broad-brimmed hats would obviously provide a more promising option. In my great grandfather's time, as is still the case today, he probably took account of the way in which the Roman Empire was expanding and realised that with increasing territory comes increasing travel, and with increasing travel comes an increasing requirement for accommodation – especially for the growing number of soldiers required to protect the Empire's newly acquired territory."

"So," enquired Plum, "I take it that one of your larger clients was, and still is, the Government of the Roman Empire?

"Yes, that is so," said Paul; "Why do you ask?"

"Oh nothing," said Plum, "I'm just curious by nature."

Although Plum was not what you might call a political animal, he was well educated and possessed an enquiring mind. From what he had gleaned from this brief period of small talk had revealed a little of Paul's position in the scheme of things and it was plain to see that, if Paul valued his livelihood, it was in his interest to keep the Roman authorities on side. It was also reasonable to conclude that Paul's business travels had broadened his outlook and developed his ability to mix with the many different people encountered on his wide-ranging business trips. An ideal position, thought Plum, from which to spread the message of Christianity. What am I thinking? This is Germany in 1940 and he is not Saint Paul. Is this what they call gaol fever and am I beginning to be as deluded as my cellmates?

The cell door swung open and in walked the guard – strangely, he looked exactly like the German guard who had ushered Plum into the cell on his arrival, but was now wearing the garb of a Roman centurion.

"There's a lady and a man here asking for Paul." said the guard; now still speaking in Greek but with a strange accent that was certainly not German. A very well-dressed couple swept into the cell.

"Ahh, Prisca and Aquila," said Paul, "you got my message; how good to see you both."

"My dearest Paul," replied Prisca, embracing him, and kissing his cheek, she went on, "How are you coping with this dreadful place? "I do hope that they will free you soon so that we can welcome you back to our home to join the many members of the church of God that you have created."

"That Christ Jesus has created," said Paul.

Luke, Demas, Epaphras and Aristarchus crowded round in excitement to join in the joyful greetings – Useful remained in the background, remembering his status as a slave. Urging Useful forward, Paul said to him,

"Come and greet our fellow workers in Christ, Prisca and Aquila."

"Well hello little fellow." said Prisca, "And what should I call you?"

"My name is Onesimus." He then, beamed as he blurted, "but my friends call me Useful."

"My name is Prisca but, some people call me Priscilla."

In the meantime, Aquila had spotted Plum standing in the shadows, watching in wonder, the reaffirmation of true and committed friendships.

"Hello there," said Aquila, with a warm smile, offering his hand, "And who might you be?"

"If you really want to know," said Plum, "I am Pelham Grenville Wodehouse...but Plum will do perfectly well."

"I'm very pleased to meet you Plum," said Aquila, shaking his hand vigorously.

"And me you," said a smiling Plum.

To have visitors – and such jolly visitors at that – after months of privation, had lifted everyone's spirits. And so, the cell buzzed with excited chatter as reminiscences were shared and news of the world outside was passed on. Then, in the absence of seating, Prisca and Aquila perched on the edge of Paul's writing table and, as they were in the same business as Paul, talked enthusiastically about such things as the current price of animal hides and the state of the world of tent making in general.

"Oh! I'd nearly forgotten the reason for me asking you to come," said Paul. "I have written a letter to the Church of God, at Corinth and wanted to ensure that it will be despatched safely."

"We will enclose it with our business correspondence," said Aquila, "and address the complete package to a trusted holy person in Jesus Christ, at Corinth, who will make sure that it reaches its destination."

"I cannot thank you enough," said Paul, embracing first Aquila and then Prisca. "May God bless you both for your assistance with this vital letter. It is my hope that it might rescue our dear brothers and sisters from taking a path that will lead them away from the salvation offered by our Lord's crucifixion."

"Please do not worry, Paul," said Prisca. "It will reach its destination safely. Our couriers are trustworthy and have never let us down."

The Guard appeared at the cell door.

"Time's up," he bellowed, "You must leave now."

Farewells were made and as the pair headed for the door Prisca cried, "Paul, how can you suffer that awful table, and that chair? We must send you some nice new ones, befitting your, position. I'll have some of my slaves drop them off for you."

"Your kind thoughts are appreciated," replied Paul, "but I would not recommend that you do, as the prison authorities will certainly appropriate them."

"Then let us hope and pray for your early release from this dreadful place," said Prisca, as she swept through the exit.

◆

"Plum," said Paul. "as you have had access to my writings, would you mind if I read some of what you have written since you have been with us?"

"Not at all, not at all, help yourself...oh, you won't be able to read it from my present writings, will you? It is in my own language…I will tell you what I will do; I will translate an excerpt from it and let you have it soon."

"Thank you, Plum, I would appreciate finding out just what it is that keeps you working away so incessantly on that machine of yours. Your ability to concentrate in such trying conditions is quite remarkable. And, whatever it is that you are writing must be of great importance."

"Don't build up your expectations in that respect, Paul. I simply happen to be a specialist in the business of writing lightweight, frothy nonsense. I love producing the stuff and the number of people who seem eager to read it would indicate that it is, in some way, beneficial to them."

"I am now so used to your disarming self-deprecation, Plum, that I do not believe a word you say in such matters and look forward to the opportunity of forming my own opinion of your literary output. Which, I am certain will prove worthwhile."

"Then I had better prepare a sizeable chunk for you to review…I don't want you to miss, through lack of adequate evidence, the genius of my weighty works…how was that for self-deprecation?"

Sometime later, Plum handed Paul a sheaf of pencil-written pages, which he had removed from one of his notepads.

"For you Paul, a wodge of my latest jocular jottings. Now in Greek. Read and, hopefully, enjoy it in good health."

"Wodge?" queried Paul. Is there such a word?"

"Probably not. I think that I just made it up – it fits though… wodge, wodge…yes, rolls of the tongue, don't you think?"

Paul began to read the opening page of Plums writings and soon became engrossed.

◆

As silence descended on the chilly, bleak cell and Plum tried to find the least uncomfortable spot on the cold, stone floor, before turning in for the night, he began to think about the extraordinary day that he had just spent with these extraordinary people. They seem to be so authentic, they never let slip their chosen identities. But what about that guard? Surely, he can't be stricken with the same delusion as the rest of them? Maybe he is being paid by the others to give authenticity to their assumed situation? And, what about Priscilla and Aquila, surely, they can't be in on it too? It might be me…maybe the strain of what has occurred throughout my time in captivity is playing tricks with my mind? I *must* stay strong. I have no alternative but to press on as best I can and act as normally as possible…if that is possible. I must cling to the fact that I am the only sane person here and make allowances for the poor deluded people with whom I am surrounded. Plum turned towards Paul:

"Paul, did you incorporate my additions in your letter?"

"In truth, I did not Plum."

"I knew that you wouldn't"

"Why?"

"I had seen the finished version several times,"

How could that be? thought Paul, mystified.

"Though," said Plum, yawning, "I did enjoy playing with it… Good night Paul."

"Good night Plum, and may God bless you."

CHAPTER TWO

A Beautiful Idea

"Plum," said Paul, "Tell me more about that man who coined the phrase, 'Common Sense...' err... Thomas somebody, wasn't it?"

"Thomas Paine?" replied Plum.

"Yes, that's him. And tell me why you think that I would not agree with what he had to say?"

"Well," said Plum, "Thomas Paine was a man from my country, Britain, who moved to live in one of its colonies, the name of which, to you, because it is so far away, will prove obscure and so we will not dwell on it. (Plum was talking about the USA but as it did not exist in Paul's time, did not wish to cause confusion). Anyway, Mr Paine had only been there a couple of years when he wrote a damning pamphlet, actually called, *Common Sense*, in which he lambasted the king of his own country, Britain – and, of course, also the king, at that time, of his newly adopted country. He called for political independence and the establishment of a republican government. The pamphlet caused a sensation, sold in great numbers and fuelled a rebellion; the upshot of which was a declaration of independence and a parting of the ways for home-country and colony."

"I see," said Paul "and now I understand why you said that I would disagree with his attitude and what he had to say."

"Having listened to you over past weeks," said Plum, "I gather that you advocate submission to civil authority on the grounds that: since all government comes from God, the civil authorities were appointed by God, and so anyone who resists authority is rebelling against God's decision, and such an act is bound to be punished?"

"Plum, I am amazed at your perception. What you have just said, I could have written myself."

(To avoid confusion, Plum had decided not to admit that he had read and heard these views several times in Paul's letter to the Romans, both in his bible at home and several times during church services).

"Paine's view," explained Plum "was that in his new country, the king is in heaven above. He maintained that: as in absolute government, the king is law, so in free countries the law ought to be king. In this respect, he really stirred things up – this boy was truly a pain to the authorities in more ways than one. He returned home to Britain and wrote another radical treatise called, *The Rights of Man*, in favour of a revolution that was taking place just across the water from Britain, in France – or, as you would call it, Gaul. And to top it all off, in another one of his mischievous ink-slinging exercises, which he called, *The Age of Reason*, he propounded deism."

"Deism...a belief in God?" queried Paul. "What is wrong with that?"

"When I said that you would not agree with what he had to say," replied Plum, "well this prime example of his bright schemes will certainly get in amongst you. I will just give you the gist of what Mr Paine means by 'deism' and leave the rest to you: according to Mr P., deism, as you say, is the belief in the existence of God; but his interpretation is based on emphasising *natural religion* as opposed to *revealed religion*...the latter being, I do believe to be your specialty."

"Well!" exclaimed Paul, "what a blessing to be living now, at a time when Christ Jesus has recently proved beyond doubt, by his glorious revelations, the truth and validity of revealed religion."

"I think I'll stop there," said Plum, "I'm feeling a little dizzy and confused."

"Oh!" said an alarmed Paul, "I hope that you are not unwell."

"I will be fine," said Plum, holding his furrowed brow. "It's only a matter of time."

"I could not help overhearing your conversation," said Luke.

"I suppose," said Paul, "that, as we coexist in a single room, such things are unavoidable."

"On that point about who should come first, God or State," continued Luke, "did not Jesus Christ give some guidance on that very question when he was up in front of Pontius Pilot? Did he not say to Pilot 'You would have no power over me if it had not been given you from above?'"

"Well," said Paul, "that tallies with my view, perfectly."

"And what about the example given by Jesus?" interjected

Aristarchus, "When he was tested by government agents devoted to the Law, on whether Jews should, or should not pay taxes to Caesar. He said, 'Give to Caesar that which is Caesar's,' surely an instruction to pay the Roman taxes?"

"I think just the opposite," said, Demas, "From what I know of that particular episode, Jesus did not answer the question posed by his interrogators but created a question of his own and answered that instead; completely wrong-footing everyone there – whether Jew or Roman – into thinking that they had received an acceptable answer."

"A clever ruse," said Plum. "For the son of a carpenter, he sounds very smart and should have been a lawyer".

"He is also the Son of God!" exclaimed Paul.

"Yes, there is that," said Plum, "It's always an advantage to have good connections."

Useful then chipped in with: "Does that mean that Jesus actually dodged the question?"

"Not in my estimation," replied Demas. "Not if you consider what Jesus actually said."

"Which was?" enquired Useful.

"If I remember correctly," said Demas, "their question was something like: 'Is it permissible for us to pay taxes to Caesar or not?' Jesus then asked them to show him a denarius. He then looked at the coin and enquired, 'Whose head and name are on it?' 'Caesar's,' they said. 'Well then,' Jesus said to them, 'Give back to Caesar which belongs to Caesar – and to God which belongs to God.'"

"Well," said Useful, "I'm with Aristarchus on this. It sounds to me like he agreed with paying taxes to Caesar."

"No, Useful, that is patently not the case," counselled Demas, "If you look closely at the answer given by Jesus, which was rhetorical."

"Which was what?" asked a baffled Useful.

"Rhet... Well, it was another question." said Demas. "Jesus answered a question with a question; and as a question is not an answer; and even if it were construed as such, it was not an answer to their original question. If studied closely, Jesus' words, 'Give back to Caesar which belongs to Caesar.' they do not stipulate what you are to give to Caesar...It leaves you open to think, I don't owe Caesar anything, but I owe all to God... and when you've given all, what is left?"

"Nothing?" queried Useful.

"Exactly," said Demas. "But what about Paul's view that we must all submit to civil authority?" Where does that leave him in this situation?"

They all turned enquiringly to Paul, who, to everyone's amazement, simply said, "It does not matter."

Luke, having begun to recover from the shock of Paul's reply, said with slightly raised voice, "Of course it matters."

"Yes," said Demas, "if Christ gives us guidance on such situations then surely it *must* matter."

"It really does *not* matter," repeated Paul.

"What do you mean by 'It does not matter?'" queried a puzzled Luke.

"Just that," said Paul, "...because the world as we know it is passing away; and so, phrases such as, 'civil authority,' will have no relevance whatsoever. It really is a waste of time and a hindrance to be taking on the Roman State when we have so little time before the coming of the Holy Kingdom."

Plum, hailing from two thousand years hence, and whose bruised mind was just recovering from Paul's earlier, seemingly, anachronistic statement concerning Thomas Paine's comment on natural religion and how fortunate it was that Christ had put paid to that argument – even before Thomas Paine was born. Plum now had to come to terms with Paul's view that the world was passing away, imminently.

On top of that, he had found all that talk about paying, or not paying taxes, had almost brought on an attack of the vapours. Only a few years previously he, himself, had had two monumental battles with the tax authorities: first those of the American Inland Revenue Service, who had attempted to relieve him of $187,000, and another, soon after, by the British Inland Revenue, who demanded £40,000. The amicable settlements moved Plum to dedicate one of his subsequent books, *Right Oh, Jeeves*, to his legal advisor, Raymond Needham KC. But still, it was verging on the traumatic to have the word 'taxes' banded about so freely.

Concerning the subject of the world's imminent passing: Plum remained safe in the knowledge that panic was completely unnecessary, as he knew for certain that they had at least two thousand years to go before bracing themselves. And that was including the time required by Adolph Hitler who, with his not-so merry men in grey, was doing his utmost to deliver Armageddon at the earliest inst. Well, thought Plum: two days, two months two years, or two thousand years is all, as Einstein would say, 'relative.' After all, what is a couple of millennia, between friends?

The others, who were used to Paul the mystic, and his enigmatic asseverations were nodding approval at what he had just said, whilst Epaphras, who had remained silent throughout the discussion, began to sing, first quietly, then with increasing volume. The others joined in and their voices rose as they began to create the most ethereal and beautiful harmonies.

When this perishable nature has put on imperishability,
And when this immortal nature has put on immortality,
Then the words of scripture will come true:
Death is swallowed up in victory.
Death, where is your victory?
Death, where is your sting?
Now the sting of death is sin,
And sin gets its power from the Law.
So let us thank God for giving us the victory
Through our Lord Jesus Christ.
Never give in then, my dear brothers,
Never admit defeat;
Keep on working at the Lord's work, always,
Knowing that, in the Lord,
You cannot be labouring in vain.

Plum sat enthralled, listening to this exceptional piece of prose poetry, now given an extra dimension by the addition of a beautiful melody. He began to think about the beauty that Christianity had brought to the world...the architecture – particularly the awe-inspiring Cathedrals; paintings; sculptures; ceramics; literature; music. Thousands upon thousands of works of great magnificence; the astonishing, never-ending flow… no, not flow, 'effusion!' of aesthetic delight and all created with enormous dedication, reverence, and love. It occurred to Plum that this man, Paul, was, himself, an artist and poet and that the interpretation contained in his concept of the true meaning of Christ's crucifixion and resurrection, and its need for preservation and development for the common good is, in itself, an astounding piece of classic art and would become the bedrock of Western culture.

It reminded Plum of the writings of one of his friends, Evelyn Waugh, who had written in his book, *Brideshead Revisited*:

> *"But my dear Sebastian, you can't seriously believe it all"*
> *"Can't I?"*
> *"I mean about Christmas and the star and the three knights*
> *and the ox and the ass."*
> *"Oh yes, I believe that. It's a lovely idea."*
> *"But you can't believe things because they're a lovely idea."*
> *"But I do. That's how I believe."*

What Paul has constructed, observed Plum, is not just a 'lovely' but a 'beautiful' Idea.' And the thought occurred to him: how could anyone be atheistic in the presence of aesthetics?

When the singing stopped, Plum, quite spontaneously, applauded.

"Bravo! Bravo!" He shouted, clapping vigorously. "What wonderful singing."

"It's one of Paul's hymns!" exclaimed Useful, excitedly.

"Yes, I know," said Plum before realising that he was not supposed to.

"How do you know that?" enquired Useful.

"Knowing the man, as I now do, I just guessed, or should I say, surmised."

Paul blushed.

♦

"Paul," said Plum, "I've been thinking."

"Do your fertile thoughts involve editing any of my epistles?"

"No, why?"

"Oh, nothing; what have you been thinking Plum?"

"Well, before I go on to tell you my latest thoughts, and as you have mentioned the recent Wodehouse humour injection, can you explain to me why you decided not to take advantage of my jocular additions to your 'Fool's Missive?' Not that I expected you to."

"The answer is quite simple, Plum. You see, the recipients of the letter would have realised, very quickly, that the style in which it was written indicated its humorous nature. It was I, Paul, who constantly reminds them that, as followers of Christ, we live through others, and not ourselves – just as Christ Jesus poured out himself for us on the cross, we offer ourselves in the service of others. For me to appear to boast about myself, in the circumstances, would have appeared to them as being so out of character that they would have found it to be hilarious. To you it might seem far too subtle, but to the members of the Church of Corinth, knowing me as they do, it would have proved uproariously funny." And I did lay the ground, as it were, by indicating early in the letter that I was talking as a fool."

"Ah! I now see what you mean," replied Plum, "I suppose I did lay my humour on with a trowel".

"Not at all Plum, you are obviously a master of your craft but for a completely different purpose – you *divert* your adherents with joyful and overt humour, and I *convert* mine with instruction disguised, in this case, as humour. Talking of which Plum, I read the part of your book which you, so kindly translated for me."

"And...dare I ask...with great trepidation, what you thought of it?"

"In truth Plum, there were lots in it that I did not understand."

"Oh, that would be my use of slang...entirely necessary when adding colour and zip to prose."

"Slang?"

"Language in common colloquial use...the kind of thing you might hear from a couple of passing centurions...extremely expressive. I sprinkle it in here and there to pep up the dialogue and, I am told, it endears my stuff to highbrow and lowbrow alike."

"The aspect of your style, Plum, that most appealed to me, is your use of simile and metaphor. It reminded me of the parables when Christ was attempting to explain the ineffable. How do you describe things that are not of this world, when mankind has created the only language you have by giving names to the things around him, here on earth? Christ Jesus talked of sheep, mustard seeds, fishers of men; anything to describe, for instance, the kingdom of heaven and its workings. What great devices metaphor and simile are for introducing graphic and emotive images. They raise consciousness above normality, and nudge the mind toward wondrous concepts. They enter a territory not achieved by direct talking but provide another vital dimension"

"You see all that in my loony scribblings?"

"I do, Plum, and it gives me just one indication – and I am sure that there are many others – of why your seemingly 'light-weight' stories carry a much deeper meaning." You transport your readers to a paradise of entirely your own making and your obvious warmth and regard for the welfare of others adds additional comfort. You provide asylum for jaded souls.

"Well, I'll be blowed, and I thought that a notable writer and poet called Hilaire Belloc, was using poetic license when he declared, publicly, that I was the best writer of English now alive. I must have spent too long in my self-created world, as I am now having difficulty believing what is being said in this one."

"Self-effacement is another of your qualities Plum…Now, after our digression, what was it you said earlier about what you have been thinking?"

"It was when I was listening to you all singing that it occurred to me that we might put that immense talent to good use."

"In what way?"

"When I think" said Plum, "of the difficulties that our fellow prisoners suffer whilst cooped up in this dreadful place, and how their thoughts must dwell upon home and loved ones, it struck me that, with such gifted people as we are presently surrounded, we might bring a little joy to each other by organising some kind of entertainment. You know? Take their minds off things for a while."

"Do you have anything in mind?"

"Well, certainly some of that impressive singing – we have an extremely gifted boy soprano in Useful."

"A boy what?"

"Oh, it's just a way we have of categorising singing voices in Britain," said Plum, (realising that, according to Paul's time, we hadn't supposed to have reached organised polyphony for another twelve hundred years.) "And we could have some kind of drama...a play... yes that is it, the play's the thing."

"A Greek tragedy!" chimed in Paul, caught up in the creative surge.

"I hardly think so," said Plum. "Aren't we supposed to be introducing a little light relief into the proceedings...a cure for home sickness and all that?"

"Oh yes, of course...I think I had better leave things to you, Plum."

"I will give the whole binge some serious thought," said Plum, "and put forward my ideas in due course."

"Binge?" More British terminology, I take it?"

"You could say that,"

"I could say that," said Paul, "but I doubt that I ever will."

"No, somehow I cannot see the word 'binge' appearing in one of your future epistles."

"Only if you were allowed to get at it, Plum."

"Shall we draw a veil?"

"I think we better had," said Paul, with a wry smile.

◆

Moving a bruised hip from a wide fissure in the large flagstone, on which he was attempting to settle for the night, Plum contemplated the day's proceedings: the conversation and debate starting with *Thomas Paine* and moving on to *God Versus the State*, which had given him pause for thought. He had to admit to mental confusion during his explanation of the exploits of Thomas Paine, one of the instigators of the parting of America from British rule. On the one hand was his allegiance to the land of his birth, Britain – one-time ruler of America – and America, itself, the home of the largest part of his readership. Britain provided his ancestry, which, in turn, had given him his aristocratic blood. He came from a long line of brave warriors who had excelled, over hundreds of years, in their military efforts for king and country. On the other hand, was his love of, and obligation to, the United States of America.

The USA, which Plum had visited for the first time in 1903, and fallen in love with, provided the bulk of his income. He appreciated his followers in the US, who had always treated him with great courtesy. Plum was torn between his criticism of Paine, the man who had been instrumental in helping to create the United States, and his allegiance to Britain, the place of his birth. Come to think of it, thought Plum, I suppose my new chum, Paul, like Thomas Paine, could be considered to be a loose cannon…or maybe, to be historically precise, a loose ballista.

I mean, thought Plum, there was Judaism tooling along quite nicely, in its orderly and organised way, for around three thousand years and along comes Jesus Christ, a Jew himself, to turn everything on its head. But to make things even more troublesome for Judaism, Paul, yet another Jew, with his genius for communication and ability to spot the brilliance of Jesus' message, wades in with his size ten sandals … (probably not size ten, as he has quite small feet …in fact he is quite a small chap in every respect except intellect.) He grasps the outstanding wisdom of a Messiah who comes – not as a warrior with a two-edged sword in his hand, ready to deal out vengeance to the oppressors – but as a bringer of peace. A Messiah who says astoundingly original things like, *love your enemy* and, *when someone strikes you, turn the other cheek.* What a neat and simple way of halting the sequence of violence begetting more violence.

Anyway, a clear parallel could be drawn between Paul and Paine. They certainly knew how to get things done. Examples being:

a) One universal religion
b) One large independent nation
c) Western civilisation
… Oh, and not forgetting,
d) A whole new culture, thrown in for good measure.

Now, this entertainment…thought Plum as he drifted off into a, hopefully, refreshing sleep.

CHAPTER THREE

Who is William Shakespeare?

" Useful! What on earth are you doing?"

Useful had the lid of Plum's suitcase open and was rummaging.

"I'm sorry Plum, but I'm dying to know what you've got in this brown box of yours."

"That brown box, as you call it, is my suitcase and as it is my property and not yours, I will thank you to keep your mischievous little hands out of it."

"He means no harm Plum," said Paul, "but, just as all small boys are curious, Useful is no different. He is not a thief."

"I know that he's not a thief," retorted Plum, "the thought never entered my mind. It's just that we suffer enough privation in here without having our personal effects handled by every passing junior miscreant."

After an awkward silence, kind-hearted Plum relented.

"Alright Useful, come on, I'll give you a quick rundown on

my meagre possessions."

Plum turned back the lid of his suitcase: "Item one," he announced, "to wit, one pair of pyjamas."

"A pair of what?" enquired a bemused Useful.

"Pyjamas," said Plum, "an Indian word, which means, in this case, nightwear."

Useful didn't know what 'Indian' meant nor, for that matter, 'nightwear' but decided to let it pass.

"That large grease spot on the bottom of the case," added Plum, "is where my wife placed a mutton chop, which I ate very soon after it was packed. And…last, but not least, the complete works of William Shakespeare."

"Is that all? "moaned a disappointed Useful.

"Well," said Plum, "the uniformed gentlemen who were, at the time, rounding me up for internment, were a little insistent that I get a move on and so that is all that I managed to put in."

"A pair of Pamajers?…" interjected Useful.

"Pyjamas," corrected Plum.

"…A stack of parchments?"

"A book" insisted Plum.

"…and a mutton chop?"

"Now a grease spot," corrected Plum, yet again.

"Hardly the sign of an organised mind Plum," said Paul, picking up the book of Shakespeare and inspecting it closely. The way it was stitched and bound; the gold-blocked letters on its cover; its deckle-edged pages.

"How have you managed to fix the individual sheets together like this?" he asked.

"Oh, I didn't do it," answered Plum, "I bought it like that."

"And the scribing," said Paul, "is so small and neat, so many words on each sheet; it is a truly wondrous thing."

"Yes," said Plum, remembering that, according to Paul and his other cellmates, Messrs Caxton and Gutenberg, Printers to the Gentry, had not yet made their appearance. "It is amazing what some people can achieve, once they put their minds to it, don't you think? You might criticise my choice of luggage content but I put it to you that those items are the sign of not only a tidy mind but also a quick-thinking mind:

a) sustenance for the body, vis. One mutton chop
b) sustenance for the mind, vis. One book…"

"A book? Is that what you call it?"
"Yes, do pay attention Paul, "and:

c) warm garments to help ensure comfortable sleep…maybe not in this hell-hole, but in more normal circumstances.

They were, beyond doubt, three essential items designed and planned to keep one in good stead, in an emergency."

"Oh, of *course* they were, Plum," said Paul, trying hard not to seem to be too patronising. "I will try to keep your strategy in mind the next time the authorities decide to lock me up again… and I feel certain that there will be a next time." He then added, "What is the 'book' about?"

"Lots of things," said Plum. "You see, it is a collection of plays by one man – they have been put together into a single volume. The writer is called William Shakespeare and he is

47

generally acknowledged as being the best playwright and poet – certainly in Britain and maybe the whole of the Western World – and in some instances, further a-field."

"Then, why have we not heard of this remarkable man?" enquired Paul.

Oh dear, here we go again, thought Plum. Little does Paul know that the work of this genius, Shakespeare, is part of (Paul's, that is) cultural legacy.

"Maybe his fame has eluded you, but cease worrying, because you are certainly aware of him now."

"But we don't know his works?"

"Maybe I could read some to you," said Plum. "The plays are written in a particular style of English which might make them a little difficult for you to read yourselves. And so, to while away some time and combat boredom, I could read you a little every day, and in so doing, provide evidence as to why this writer is held in such high esteem."

By now, everyone in the cell had gathered round to listen to what seemed to be an increasingly interesting conversation, now developing into a welcomed opportunity for an entertainment-starved prison populace.

"Oh Plum," exclaimed, Epaphras, "would you please read some to us? I would really enjoy that".

Everyone nodded in agreement.

"Yes, I think we would all like that," confirmed Paul. "When will you start?"

"Whenever you can all find it convenient," said Plum.

"Now!" cried Useful, jumping up and down excitedly.

Paul interjected, "I'm sorry Useful, but I have some letters to write and I, like you, do not want to miss any of Plum's reading. So, do you all mind waiting a little while, until then?"

"Oh, all right," said Useful discontentedly, "but you're always writing letters, Paul."

"Useful," said Plum, "do try to have a little patience. Paul's letters are more important than you will ever know, and the odd hour of your time is little to ask. After all, remember that a lot of Paul's letter writing involves spreading the Good News."

"Yes, you're right Plum," said Useful, brightening. "Very well Paul, scribe away."

"I have your permission then, Useful? Good." said Paul, with a smile.

◆

With Paul's letters written, everyone settled down to enjoy their first experience of this miraculous man, William Shakespeare.

"Now, what would you like," Plum asked, opening the book, "comedy or drama?"

Surprisingly, considering the dire situation they were in, the majority chose drama.

"Now let me see, there are some that have ghosts in them, what about one of those?"

"Yes!" was the general cry – especially from Useful, who obviously had a penchant for ghosts and was in danger of exploding from excitement. And so, it came to be a daily oasis of pleasure for all as they gathered round Plum, made themselves as comfortable as possible on the hard floor and settled in for a slice of Hamlet. Even the guard, Fritz-cum-Markus, made sure he was checking their cell at that time and managed to hover about until the reading had finished. Plum overcame the language difficulty as he cleverly translated and paraphrased simultaneously.

After several sessions, Plum came to the end of his serialised Hamlet and all agreed that it had been a good story, well read. Paul told Plum that he was impressed with Shakespeare's understanding of human beings and their many foibles.

"That is what we call, the 'Human Condition'" explained Plum.

"That is an excellent description," said Paul, "and it reminds me of some of the difficulties I have, when dealing with some of our church members."

"Such problems," said Plum, "provide the basis of one of the main themes of that particular play. Hamlet is constantly wrestling with the difficulty of making sound decisions based upon his perception of what the people around him are telling him. People are so complex that they have private reasons for how they conduct themselves whilst in the company of others – usually a complication caused by insecurity, low self-esteem, or just plain fear of loss of face. They feel a need to defend themselves and can become motivated by jealousy, envy, greed, vanity, revenge, or any number of emotions. This can result in their being evasive when answering what seems to be a quite innocuous question. It seems that human beings are more prone to emotion that logic. And, no matter how you try to convince them of a logical approach to achieving a particular goal, they can prove suspicious and divisive."

"Yes, Plum, what you have said…"

"What William Shakespeare has demonstrated," Plum interjected, "...has helped clarify," continued Paul, "situations that have been puzzling me for years. I am aware of the occasional duplicity of my fellow man – especially those in our churches. Jealousy, contention, abuse and wicked mistrust, are just some of the problems I have attempted to counter. I constantly remind them to leave no room for selfish ambition or vanity and to look to each other's interests and not merely their own. But your Mr Shakespeare has helped in crystallising my thinking on such matters. I suppose," continued Paul, "that, as we cannot actually get into the minds of those around us, we have the difficulty of trying to perceive what they really mean when they speak. We can't ever guarantee that we are hearing the precise truth, but just have to make our decisions on what we perceive they actually mean."

"Yes," said Plum, "it puts an entirely different complexion on existing with those around us."

"Maybe Pontius Pilot was in a similar quandary," said Luke, "when he said, 'Truth, what is that?' He did not realise that he was gazing into the face of Christ Jesus, the divine man put on this earth to speak only the truth. Truth personified was literally staring Pilot in the face."

"Yes," said Plum, "and look where it got Jesus."

"Ha!" said Paul, "But look where it has got us".

"In gaol?" queried Plum.

"NO!" shouted an exasperated Paul.

"I know, I know," said Plum. "It's just that I could not resist the opportunity of procuring a laugh. It's a doubtful habit, I know."

Useful then brought the matter to a close with a timely interruption.

"Plum," he said, pulling on Plum's sleeve.

"Hullo!"

"I really did enjoy the story about Hamlet."

"I'm very pleased to hear it young Useful. Did you find it instructive?"

"Oh yes – especially the ghost. That was really creepy."

"Creepy? Well I'm sure that Mr Shakespeare would be very pleased to know that. He prided himself on 'Creepy,' among other things, of course."

"But…" said Useful, hesitantly, "the bits when Hamlet was talking to himself for ages…"

"Oh, the soliloquies?" said Plum.

"…is that what they call them?" enquired Useful, distractedly.

"Yes," said Plum, "they are, for me, some of the most revealing parts."

"Well…" said Useful, hesitantly, "I don't want to upset you Plum, because it was very good of you to read for us, and I want you to do it again…but…"

"Come on, oh small freckled one, spit it out?"

"Well, I found them really boring."

"Useful, you are a genius!" exclaimed Plum, leaping to his feet.

"Am I?"

"You certainly are you miniature brainwave instigator."

"Are you pleased because you have a miniature brain and I've done something to it?" enquired a still puzzled Useful.

"Well I do have a mini… but that is beside the point. You

have given me an idea for our entertainment. Paul! Come and listen to what Useful has provided for us?"

Paul, who had by then moved away, came over.

"Paul," said Plum, elatedly, "I have been wracking my brain about what we might do as part of our evening – or daytime for that matter – of entertainment and Useful here has given me a great idea."

Useful stood there beaming and feeling particularly proud; but for what, he wasn't at all sure.

"Let me explain," said Plum.

"I wish you would," said Useful, eager to know why he was a declared genius.

"Useful was telling me that he found Hamlet's soliloquies to be boring."

"Well," said Useful, "they're so sad and miserable."

"Exactly!" said Plum", and it was that that reminded me of a play in three short and manageable tabloids, which should prove ideal for inclusion in our evening's entertainment. It was a play that I took part in whilst at school and, wonder of wonders, it is a comedy based around the soliloquies of Hamlet. It's called Rosencrantz and Guildenstern and was written by a very funny gentleman called W. S. Gilbert. I cannot remember all the words to it, but I do remember the plot very well indeed; so well that I shall attempt to write a version of it. And, as we are now all familiar with Shakespeare's original version, we should be able to appreciate the humorous intentions of Mr Gilbert who, like Useful, must have found the soliloquies really tedious."

"And boring," insisted Useful.

"And, Useful, as you would have it, 'boring,'" echoed a jubilant Plum.

◆

During one of his heavy sessions at the typewriter, Plum was approached by the prison guard (the one with a predilection for dressing up but this time, surprisingly, back in his German army uniform). He addressed Plum:

"Herr Wodehouse".

"Hullo!" replied Plum, without taking his eyes from his typing.

"I am informed that you are arranging some sort of entertainment. Is that correct? And, to be performed by some of the people in this cell?"

"Yes, that is so," said Plum. "It is based around Shakespeare's Hamlet."

"Oh, Shakespeare," said the guard delightedly "I am a great admirer of the work of your brilliant Countryman and I really enjoyed your readings – I tried not to miss any of them."

"I am truly flattered," replied Plum (pleased to be talking to someone from the twentieth century), "and I'm sure that, had he still been alive, Bill would be too."

"Bill…?" queried a very puzzled Fritz.

"What was it that you wanted to ask me Frit… do you know? I have not yet learned your name?"

"Rudigar Dressler," said the guard, "but I am better known as Rudi."

"And I, Rudi, am called Plum"

"Yes, I know Herr Plu…Wodehouse," blurted Rudi, "because I have read and enjoyed lots of your books. I really would like to be in the play you are preparing. Do you think that you could find me a part? I promise I will work very hard to make my performance as good as it could possibly be to give you complete satisfaction."

"I'm not yet at the casting stage," answered Plum, "but, when I am, do you not think that I should give my fellow captives their opportunities first?"

"I know, I know, I know," said a now fervent and anguished Rudi,

"but, Herr Wodehouse, I have always wanted to act in a drama and it would mean so much to me…I will even provide my own costume."

"I somehow thought you might," said Plum, whilst thinking to himself, it is probably in the same dressing-up box as your Roman centurion outfit.

"I cannot promise anything but will definitely keep you in mind." said Plum, adopting the air of a theatrical agent.

"Oh, danke, danke, danke Herr Wodehouse," said a very grateful Rudi, shaking Plum's hand vigorously.

"Bitte, bitte, bitte," answered Plum, and to retain the theatrical agent motif, went on: "If there should be a vacancy, I promise that you will be the first thespian to whom I turn."

Not comprehending the word 'thespian' Rudi looked mystified, before strutting away, scratching his head, which proved ineffective, as he was wearing a tin helmet.

◆

After a few days of hard thinking and furious typing, Plum finished his approximation of the W.S. Gilbert play, *Rosencrantz and Guildenstern*, before turning his attention to the creation of a running order for the whole of the intended event. Thus far, he had the play, which he considered would take up the whole of the second half; and two very fine hymns – to be beautifully sung by the P.C.A.S.C.E. or, as he had decided to call them, the 'Prison Cell Appreciation Society, Choral Ensemble' – which could be used to open and close the first half; but what about the section between those hymns? That aspect needed further consideration. We have culture with our hymns, recounted Plum, and some cod-culture with our mock Shakespeare; and so, what about a little overt popular culture? Oh, if only I had my banjolele, I could have given them a medley of jazz and minstrel tunes. *Now* that gives me an idea for one item – short and sweet…but amusing thought Plum, jotting it down.

Having – thanks to Useful's prompting – rediscovered the Shakespeare lampoon from his school stage performance, Plum revisited, in thought, that same period to see if there might be other possible items for use in the show.

"Ha yes!" Exclaimed Plum, loudly – making the other cell members jump with fright.

"Sorry gentlemen," he said, to his wide-eyed cohabiters, "I, too, was taken by surprise but in my case, by the muse."

Song of Hybrias The Cretan, thought Plum. That might do. Back at his alma mater, Dulwich College, in the environs of South London, when but a youth, Plum had been given a mention in his school newssheet for his stirring rendition during the school concert, of this ancient drinking song. Nostalgia

56

gripped as he struck a heroic pose and began to sing in a rich bass baritone:

"My wealth's a burley spear and brand,
And a right good shield of hides untanned
And a right good shield of hides untanned
Which on my arm I buckle."

The outburst caused further disquiet among the local populace. Some feared for his mental wellbeing, whereas others, because he was singing the blood-thirsty ditty in English, thought him in the thrall of the Spirit and speaking in tongues. Plum continued:

"With these I plough, I reap, I sow,
With these I plough, I reap, I sow,
With these I plough, I reap I sow
With these I make the sweet vintage grow
And all around me truckle..."

All around him did not truckle, but Plum continued to baffle.

"It is a song that I sang as a youth," he explained. "I was giving it an airing with the intention of brushing it up for inclusion in our entertainment. I thought it might suit because it was written by an ancient Greek poet called Hybrias and is called the 'Spear Song'."

"It didn't sound very Greek to me," said Useful.

"That might be because I sang it in my own language," retorted Plum, "but I will translate it into Greek for my performance, if you approve."

"We'll give it a listen later and let you know," said Useful, cheekily.

"I know a poem by Hybrias that has a spear mentioned in it," said Demas… "let me see if I can remember any of it…oh yes…it goes something like,

'My riches are spear and sword and beautiful shield…But those who do not dare to bear spear and sword and the beautiful shield that protects the body fall all down unto their knees with awe and address me as Lord and great King.'"

"That is the source from which the Spear Song has been taken," said Plum."

"Just give me a spear and a sword and a beautiful shield!" Exclaimed Useful, lunging and parrying, with an imaginary sword, as if in battle, "I'll show you how it's done."

"You are a slave, Useful. Retorted Demas, "You are confined to the household. It is not for you to go out into the world to seek glory."

Useful's head fell to his chest in despair before rising again as he cried triumphantly, "I will, I will…one day…go out into the world, not to seek glory but to spread glory…the glory of Christ Jesus."

"Well said Useful!" exclaimed an excited Paul. "Well said indeed."

"But he never will," grizzled Demas. "How can a lowly slave, owned by his master take part in great public events and make his way in the world. What kind of future is that? If I were in such a position, I would do away with myself."

"You disappoint me Demas," said Paul, fuming like a volcano on the verge of eruption. You call yourself a follower of Christ and harbour the thoughts of a heretic. You worry too much about your situation here on earth and what you can get out of it for your own selfish gratification. Not a thought do you possess of attaining the Kingdom of God!"

Even Plum, whose blood usually remained cool to tepid during the most daunting of trials, was moved by Demas' utterances to boiling point, "Do you think that Useful chose his situation himself? Courage is not confined to the free – and God knows this boy has provided enough evidence of his great courage whilst in our presence. I suspect that your own love for life and self-preservation would deter you from any enterprise that involved glory or courage. Do away with yourself indeed. Why, with your attitude, count yourself as already dead!"

A stunned silence pervaded the cell for some time until, eventually, Plum, sat down upon his typewriter case and began to peruse his running order for the show.

ITEM	PERFORMER(S)
1. Hymn	P.C.A.S.C.E.
2. Song of Hybrias The Cretan	Plum
3. Novelty song	TBA
4. Item required.	TBA
5. Hymn	P.C.A.S.C.E.

INTERVAL

1. Rosencrantz & Guildenstern Cast to be selected

END

We require something of about ten minutes' duration to fill the number four slot, thought Plum. He decided to leave that item for the time being, in the expectation that an idea would eventually suggest itself.

◆

As the cellmates lay there in the dark, attempting to get some sleep, the silence was broken:

"Paul, I've been thinking," said Useful.

"Ooh this sounds ominous," said Plum.

"Well," continued Useful, "it's when Paul is teaching us about The Good News and the new covenant given to us by God, through Jesus."

"What is it that is troubling you Useful?" queried Paul.

"Well…if we believe that God is perfect, how is it that he had to replace the first covenant? Surely, being perfect, he would have got the covenant right in the first place. Having to change it is like admitting that he got it wrong."

"Out of the mouths of babes," said Plum.

"I have had this same question from some of our church members," said Paul, "not in the same words as used by Useful but, none the less, raising the same subject and voicing their difficulty in coming to terms with what appears to be a contradiction."

"And what did you tell them?" asked a very curious Useful.

"I will try to make it as simple as I can for you," said Paul.

"And for me too," said Plum (who had read Paul and was aware of what he had written but felt the need to give support to Useful).

"God is perfect," continued Paul, "have no doubts of that. But, the problem is that mankind certainly is not. God gave mankind the freedom to make their own way by making their own decisions. But to help them in their formative years, he created the first covenant, initially with Abraham and subsequently with Moses at Mount Sinai, where he reinforced it by setting out in detail, the relationship between God and Jews. Those early covenants were mankind's guardian until the Christ came, when mankind could be justified by faith alone. Having the first and second covenants, as given to Abraham and Moses, can be likened to having a servant whose duty it is to take a child to school – to make sure that the child suffers no harm and is delivered safely to its place of learning. It was on being placed into the charge of its teacher that the child's learning really began in earnest."

"But not all followers of Christ are Jews," said Useful, "Me for one…I'm not a Jew."

"Then you, Useful," said Paul, "are one of the beneficiaries of the new covenant given to us by Christ Jesus, the son of God. Through your belief in Christ, you have received the spirit."

"Me too," said Plum, nodding enthusiastically.

"Yes, and you too Plum," said a smiling Paul; "because Jesus saw no differences in anyone. Regardless of race, class, or gender, if you believe in Christ Jesus, you will have a place in God's Kingdom."

"No rules then?" Useful asked.

"Just two," said Plum, "Love God with all your heart and soul and love your neighbour as yourself."

"Well, that sounds easy," said a jubilant Useful.

"Oh, is that so?" said Plum, "Loving God is the easy part; it's the neighbours' part that we have to really worry about."

"With all their Shakespearian foibles," laughed Paul.

"You've got it, Paul," said Plum; "but we will just keep on loving that neighbour whether he likes it or not."

"Then, in that case, you too have got it, Plum," said Paul, grinning.

Chuckles echoed around the cell as the other inmates appreciated the joy in what they had just heard.

CHAPTER FOUR

The Naming of Parts

P lum asked everyone in the cell if they would kindly gather-round him. As they settled themselves in a semi-circle on the floor, all were curious as to what he was about to say.

"I would appreciate your assistance with the contents of our entertainment."

There was a murmur of interest and expectation.

"I have prepared a list of items, that, subject to your approval, might provide a divers and amusing theatrical presentation."

"Do you mean our show?" chirruped Useful.

"Useful," replied Plum, "you have a gift for the succinct. Yes, I mean our show."

Plum read to them his suggested running order, which gained general approval, and then continued.

"As you will have noticed, I require your help with item number four. Try as I may, I cannot come up with anything that might fit that part of the proceedings."

"Why don't we explore the individual talents within our own group?" said Demas. "We might find the solution here?"

"An excellent idea," said Plum. "Suggestions anyone?"

"I saw a man in the market place once," said Useful, enthusiastically...

"*He is* not in our group though, is he?" retorted Demas.

"But let me finish!" exclaimed Useful.

"Yes, let him finish," said Paul.

"This man was bound in chains," continued Useful, "and people were then asked to check that the chains and locks were real...then," said Useful, dramatically, "he was placed into a sack and...

"And then," interjected Demas, "the centurions dragged him away, and that's how he came to be in this cell with us."

"No!" exclaimed, Useful. "Paul! Will you tell him to stop interrupting me?"

Paul smiled patiently at Demas who, looking amused, shrugged his shoulders and smiled back at him.

"Anyway," said Useful, with wide-eyed excitement, "within minutes, Maranatha!..."

"Maranatha!" echoed the cellmates.

"the man leapt out of the sack and was completely free of his locks and chains!"

There was a stunned silence as everyone waited for the next 'Useful' utterance.

"Escapologist," said Plum.

"Eh?" queried the cellmates.

"An escapologist," repeated Plum. "That is what we Britain's call those people who pop in and out of things – sometimes in

64

shackles and then, as you would have it, 'Maranatha!' out of shackles. The most famous being a chap called Houdini, who performed the most extraordinary feats. One of which entailed being shackled from head to foot before being lowered – upside down, I'll have you know – into a brimming tank of water, where he remained until the audience was sure he must have drowned, and was becoming increasingly distressed. Then out he leapt, free of his shackles, as if he had just been for a refreshing dip! Houdini was such a master of the art of escapology – he even escaped from a secured prison cell – that he said that after his death he would escape death and return to life."

"Coo," gurgled Useful, eyes bulging.

"Returning from the dead is an occurrence reserved by God for only one person and that is Christ Jesus," remarked Paul. "And, Useful, I hardly consider, 'Maranatha!' to be an appropriate word to use when surprised by the reappearance of a theatre magician. That, too, is best reserved for the reappearance of Jesus Christ himself."

"Does it not mean, 'Come, O Lord?'" queried Plum.

"Yes, it *does*," Paul asserted, firmly.

"Never mind Useful." said a sympathetic Plum. "There is a word I can give you that, in Britain, we use for such occasions."

"What's that Plum?"

"Ta dah!!!" sang Plum. "Oh, that is two words, is it not?"

"What's that again, Plum?"

"Ta dah!!!" Trumpeted Plum.

"Ta dah!!! Ta dah!!! Ta dah!!!" sang Useful, thrilled with his new phrase.

"Where is all this getting us with our search for another item for our show?" queried Aristarchus.

"Yes, what *is* the point of your story?" asked Paul of Useful.

"Well...I thought," replied Useful... "if I really practiced very hard..."

The cellmates groaned in unison.

... "I could be a great escallopologist," insisted Useful.

"Yes," said Plum, "I am sure you could, should you take up heraldry or seafood cookery."

Paul suggested that Useful might practice the art of escape and if, by the time of the show, he had reached, what he himself considered to be the required standard, he might then demonstrate his newly honed skills in the show.

"Considering his present situation," Plum remarked, "It is understandable that the boy should harbour such ambitions as learning how to escape."

"In that case," said Demas, gesturing with his thumb, "I suggest, Useful, that you start by honing your skills with the lock on that large cell door."

"In the meantime," suggested Plum, "if Useful is our plan A, let us, to be on the safe side, put our thoughts to a plan B."

Silence prevailed, until broken by Plum.

"Some years ago," he said, "I was employed in the business of musical comedy and when a situation, or what we called, 'a bug,' arose – similar to the one with which we are now faced – the usual panacea suggested by our impresario was to 'Bring on the Girls.' The 'girls' comprised a dance troupe who would give their all in the art of Terpsichore and, invariably, save the show."

"In case you hadn't noticed," said Epaphras, "there are no girls in here."

"That is a shame," said Demas.

"Steady," said Paul.

"But," said Plum, "we might not have girls, but we may have people who can dance."

"What kind of dances might we do?" enquired Aristarchus.

"What kind do you know how best to perform?" enquired Plum.

"There are lots of traditional Jewish dances," said Paul.

"And from what I remember from my attendance at the weddings of some of my Jewish friends," said Plum, "the dances can be very stirring and promote great excitement – just the kind of thing we need for our show."

"Yes," said Luke, "but each dance symbolises something taking place at a particular moment in a ceremony. If taken out of context, it could appear strange to those to whom the traditional dances are familiar."

"Well then, we will appoint the one amongst us deemed to be the most gifted as a dancer, to be our choreographer."

"Our what?" enquired about a third of those present, with the others just settling for being puzzled.

"A choreographer," explained Plum, "is a person who decides what dance moves and steps are to be incorporated into the creation of, what we people in musical comedy refer to as, a routine. I suggest that our appointed choreographer takes moves and steps from traditional Jewish dances to create a new dance routine – one that will last for a specified amount of time, to suit the needs of our show. In that way, we will have recognisable steps and moves that, whilst being reminiscent of Jewish traditional dance, do not detract from their original purpose."

This resulted in the Jewish members of the company, Paul among them, trying out a few deft moves as they hopped from foot to foot and swirled around the cell.

"That's the spirit!" exclaimed Plum, keeping a sharp eye out for a potential choreographer.

◆

When, eventually, the hubbub began to subside, Plum addressed them once again:

"Now that we have a format for our show, there is another important aspect with which I will require your help."

"Yes, of course Plum," said Paul, "just explain to us your requirements and we will assist in any way that we can."

The others nodded their eager agreement. Plum continued:

"I have now written a version of the play, *Rosencrantz and Guildenstern*, which, for expediency's sake, I used my typewriter. But, because it has the Roman and not the Greek alphabet, we now need to produce copies of my script for use by all those taking part, but, in the language that we all understand: Greek."

"How can we help with that?" enquired Luke.

"I suggest," replied Plum, "that, for a manageable period each day, I dictate my script to those among you who are able to take dictation. That seems to me to be the quickest method by which to produce the required number of copies to fulfil the needs of our cast."

"But," said a perturbed Useful, "I can't read or write, so how will I learn what to say?"

"You don't yet know that you are actually in the play," said

Demas. "So maybe, that problem won't arise."

"Oh Plum," pleaded Useful, "I am going to be in it aren't I …I've got to be…oh *please*."

"That brings me to the matter of casting," said Plum.

"Are you going to cast something at Useful… like a big wet rag," chortled Demas.

"Demas! rebuked Paul. "Leave the child alone. Your treatment of him is quite mean-spirited at times – as well as unbecoming of a follower of Christ."

"Sorry Paul," replied a chastened Demas, "I was only having a little fun."

"Casting, in this instance, Demas," interjected Plum, "means choosing suitable people to fulfil each role in the show. So, let us go through the characters in the play and put names to roles. Now, item one: which is one of Paul's' hymns – well, that looks after itself does it not? They will, I trust, be sung by all, as when I first heard you, soon after my arrival at this barbarian boarding house.

Item two: *Song of Hybrias the Cretan* – to be sung by a fine, strapping young bass-baritone. Mmm now who can that be? Oh, it's me! As I have now translated the song into Greek, I will run it by you when we start rehearsals, in the hope that once you appreciate the rousing lyric, you will take it to your hearts – but please resist the temptation to join in on the peppy bits. It is, after all, a solo item.

Now…item three," continued Plum: "A Novelty Song… Back in Britain, about a decade ago, there was a song that took my country by storm. It is a cheesy bit of nonsense involving a father who sings to his young son. It is called Sonny Boy, has a likeable melody and – as the boy perches on his father's knee throughout the performance, whilst his besotted Pop sings to him in a heart-rending manner – is also visually interesting. I suggest that Useful, being the youngest member of our crew, should play the part of the knee-dandled, Sonny Boy."

"I'll do that," piped Useful, in his, predictably, enthusiastic manner.

"Excellent," said a pleased Plum. "Now, is there any amongst you who would like to take the part provided by Sonny Boy's wailing Pa?"

Dead silence.

"Mmm," uttered Plum, "that is disappointing. I'm sure that if played and sung well, this item would add to the rich texture of our production. I would hate to drop it ...looks as if I will have to think further on that one. Moving on then, to item four: The Dance Routine."

"I think we all want to take part in that," said Paul, shimmying just a little.

The others nodded enthusiastically, with some already beginning to sway and hop around.

"Having observed you all," continued Plum, "since recommending this seemingly popular item, it looks to me – and I hope you will agree – that Epaphras seems to have a natural gift for, not only music but rhythmical movement."

"Do you mean dancing?" chirruped Useful.

"You have it in one Useful," replied Plum, "and I nominate Epaphras as our choreographer."

Epaphras looked coy and a little embarrassed by the attention so suddenly directed his way. There was a buzz of general approval of Plum's suggested choice.

"Please raise your hand if you agree," said Plum, "that Epaphras should become our choreographer?"

The choice proved popular, as every hand, (with some raising two), was eagerly waved aloft.

"Well, Epaphras," enquired Plum, "Will you agree with our unanimous choice?"

As Epaphras nodded his agreement, the spontaneous cheer that followed almost rattled the lock on the door (the same lock that had taken up so much of Useful's time recently, as he kept slipping away to pursue his new vocation as an escapologist).

"As a fitting finish to the first half of our show," announced Plum, "we have item five, which is another of Paul's Hymns, to be sung by the choir. Which, as I said earlier, when planning item one, looks after itself. Now, as suggested by Demas, we are looking for talent amongst our own number for use in the show. Do we have any people who can play an instrument?"

"I can play the lyre," said Epaphras.

"And I the timbrel," said Luke,

"Excellent!" exclaimed a delighted Plum.

"But," said Epaphras, "I do not have a lyre with me."

"Nor I a timbrel," said Luke.

"It's the same with my banjolele," said a disconsolate Plum. On reflection, he mused quietly to himself, it would have proved a better choice for packing than the mutton chop…and, as an extra bonus; I would not now have a grease spot in my suitcase.

"I'm sure," suggested Paul, "that if I wrote to Prisca and Aquila they would acquire the necessary instruments, and bring them to us."

"Oh, that would be absolutely capital Paul," said a brightening Plum. "Would you kindly do so? Now on to the second half of our show; and casting for the play. I have prepared a dramatis personae; and as I read out the names of each character we will try to agree on who is to play whom. In order of their appearance we have: QUEEN, who can take that?"

Silence prevailed.

"What seems to be the problem?" enquired Plum.

"Well," said Luke, a little embarrassed, "she's...a woman."

"Naturally?" queried Plum, "Queens usually are."

"But we are not women," Luke replied.

"When Shakespeare wrote his plays," said Plum, "one of which, this play is based upon, all women's parts were played by men. In his day, there were no female actors; so, you could say that by using all male actors we are adding authenticity to our production."

Dead silence now prevailed.

"I would take this part myself," ventured Plum, "but it is my intention, with your approval, to play the part of Guildenstern, with which I am already familiar, having played it before, when at school."

Even deader silence (if that were possible).

"We had better move on then," said Plum, "in the hope that we can solve this problem later. The next character is CLAUDI-US the King."

The showing of hands resembled that of the vote for Epaphras to take the post of choreographer – only, this time, more people raised both hands. It was reminiscent of the class swat, hand stiffly raised, trying to catch the eye of the teacher who had asked the whole class for an answer to a question. Please sir, please sir, me sir! Me sir!

"Now," said Plum, "that is better."

"Maybe," suggested Aristarchus, "on reflection, as he is our natural leader, Paul is best suited for the part of King?"

"Don't entertain such thoughts," said Paul incredulously.

"Remember your words as you emerged from your baptismal water – 'No more Jew or Greek, slave or freeman, male or female!'" Paul then added, "We are all equal in Christ Jesus."

"There is another aspect, Aristarchus," said Plum; "the King in this play is afforded very little dignity. In fact, a large part of the comedy is based upon subjecting him to ridicule. Nevertheless, a professional actor would not let his dignity or personal image enter into his choice of a part," (except in Hollywood, thought Plum to himself).

"I would like to play that King," said Paul. "Christ offered a glorious example of how to bear ridicule and derision with great dignity; and I, myself, have first-hand experience of such treatment. Given the opportunity, I would relish the role."

"Good for you Paul," said Plum. "And what about the rest of us? Do we agree that Paul should play the King?"

The whole company nodded enthusiastically.

"Well, that's that settled," said an extremely pleased Plum. "The next character up is GUILDENSTERN," he continued, "and, for the reason given earlier, I would like to apply for that particular part. If you had read in my school newssheet, *The Alleynian*, the notices, regarding my performance, you would not hesitate in granting my application. The fact," he added, with a twinkle, "that I was one of that newssheet's editors at the time had no bearing on the matter, whatsoever."

Also, twinkling, the company agreed, to a man.

"My heartfelt thanks, gentlemen," said Plum. "Now, onto the question of which of you might play ROSENCRANTZ."

"Do they treat him like they do the king?" said Useful, "You know...make fun of him?"

"No, they do not," said Plum, "in fact he gets to make fun of, not only the king but Hamlet too."

"Then, I'll take that part," said Useful.

"But he is a fully-grown man, Useful," said Plum, "it will be difficult for you to have conviction in the part and to convince the audience that you are who you are supposed to be."

"I *could* do it!" said a resolved Useful.

"Useful, my small, but beautifully marked messmate," said Plum, "I think that we should see if we can find another part in this play, more suited to your stature."

"Oh, all right then, Plum, carry on," said a reassured Useful.

"I'll take the part," said Demas.

"Is everyone happy that Demas should take the part of Rosencrantz?" asked Plum.

As there were no objections, Plum took it as a yes and wrote Demas' name against that of Rosencrantz, on his list.

"Now, on to the character, OPHELIA."

"That sounds like a girl's name," said Useful.

"It, or should I say, *she* is, a girl," answered Plum.

"Well, we're not being girls, are we?" said Useful, to all those around him.

"Useful," said Plum, encouragingly, "I think, with your diminutive stature, this part will suit you admirably."

"I'm not going to be a girl!" shouted Useful, petulantly, "I will look ridiculous!"

"Useful," said Demas persuasively, "you know what Paul said about ridicule, and the way that it has to be borne with dignity; and how he and Jesus have faced it with fortitude. Paul took the part of the ridiculed king to show how he can bear humiliation for the sake of a worthwhile cause…and surely our show is just that?"

"Oh, all right then," said Useful, "if Jesus and Paul can do it, then so can I."

"Bless you Useful," said Paul, patting him, affectionately, on his tousled head. Useful beamed, as his name was placed on Plum's list, against that of Ophelia.

"That," said Plum, "takes us on to HAMLET. Any takers?"

Luke, Aristarchus and Epaphras, who had not yet received parts in the play, raised their hands simultaneously.

"There are three of you," said Plum, "but only one part remaining – unless in the light of what has recently transpired, someone would now like to play the role of the Queen, then there are two parts available."

The trio of would-be performers stood shuffling their feet and looking embarrassed.

"All right then, we had better draw straws for who is to take the part of Hamlet," said a disappointed Plum.

"We have no straws," piped Useful.

Paul then came up with the suggestion that, as they varied in length, they use some of his quill pens; he grasped a bunch of three, made a fist and offered them to the waiting trio. Luke was declared the victor.

"Well," said Plum, "that concludes the casting for the play – except for the Queen."

At that point, the cell door opened noisily and in came Rudi, the guard, muttering about there being something jammed in the keyhole.

"I'm just checking the cell," he said, disingenuously, (he had guessed that they might be choosing people for the play and thought that he might do a little eavesdropping).

"Ah Rudi!" Exclaimed Plum, eyes gleaming, "I am so glad you came."

"Are you?" replied an expectant Rudi, whose eyes now out-gleamed Plum's,

"Is there something you want me to do, Herr Wodehouse?"

"It's that we have a part in our play," said Plum, nonchalantly, "that is proving too difficult for the actors at my disposal…and I wondered…"

"Yes, yes, yes, I will, Herr Plu…Wodehouse, oh certainly, certainly, certainly."

"Good, good, good," replied Plum.

"Whom, do you want me to play? said an eager Rudi, "Hamlet? King Claudius? Rosencrantz?"

"The Queen!" announced Plum, resisting the urge to place his fingers in his ears as he awaited the reply.

"The Queen!" bellowed Rudi, raising both hands to his face. "The Queen? The Queen? The Queen?"

"The Queen, The Queen, The Queen, indeed," said Plum querulously, not knowing if Rudi was appalled or pleased at the offer.

"The part I was hoping for!" screeched an almost hysterical

Rudi. "I have just the dress for it!"

"And, I just knew that you would have, Herr Dressler,"

"Oh danke, danke danke, Herr Wodehouse."

"On the contrary, Herr Dressler, it's danke, danke danke to you for being so gracious in agreeing to take the part."

"It is entirely my pleasure Herr Wodehouse; I cannot wait to finish my duties and to get home to try out my dress... with my part in mind, of course."

"Of course, of course of course," said Plum.

Rudi then hyperventilated for a time before gasping..."the... Queen!"

"Well," said Plum, "that really does complete our casting for the play. And, Epaphras, it is probably a blessing that you are not acting in it, as it will leave you free to play the lyre when music is required as indicated in the script. You also have more than enough to do with your responsibility as choreographer and musical accompanist for the dance sequence. Aristarchus, beside your taking part in the dance sequence, I would appreciate your close observance of rehearsals for the play. You can be our understudy, in the eventuality that someone might have to drop out due to some unforeseen circumstance. And, as I have some experience of the theatre, would anyone mind if I take the rôle as director of the whole production?"

Everyone nodded enthusiastically.

"As you would say, Plum," said Paul; "That looks after itself."

"When do we start the rehearsals?" enquired, Aristarchus.

"After we have prepared our scripts for the play," replied Plum. "Oh! and I will have to think about a replacement for the Sonny Boy item."

"Sonny Boy item...vas ist?" queried Rudi, regaining his composure.

"Oh, it is a song I had in mind for the first half of the show," said Plum with mock distraction, "we have a Sonny Boy but no one to sing the part of his father."

"Climb upon my knee, sonny boy,"

Sang Rudi, in English, clutching his hands to his chest.

"Although you're only three, sonny boy!"

"You know the song then?" asked Plum.

"Oh yah!" Exclaimed Rudi, "It was very popular in my country about twelve years ago, before Herr Hitler came to power... Al Jolson, we all loved his singing.

"Mammy how I love ya, how I love ya, my dear old Mammy!"

Warbled Rudi, with flailing hands and contorted features.

"Then Rudi," said Plum, "would you mind singing Sonny Boy in the show?"

"Not at all, Herr Wodehouse but I will have to think about what to wear."

"What about a black dinner suit and white gloves?" suggested Plum.

"Perfect, perfect, perfect," said Rudi, "I have just such an outfit."

"Of course you have," said a delighted Plum.

"Do you want me to black my face, Herr Wodehouse?" burbled Rudi.

"I'd rather you didn't," said Plum, I think you'll be fine in all your chubby pinkness."

"Herr Wodehouse, you wish me to apply makeup?"

"Sparingly, please Rudi, sparingly" requested Plum.

◆

Evening found Plum lying on his stone mattress (a.k.a. the floor), thinking about this and that, when Paul spoke to him.

"Plum?"

"Hullo."

"I was surprised and interested, to find that you and the prison guard seem to have something in common."

"I suppose we probably have. When taking into consideration the size of the Roman Empire, we are almost neighbours. I, as you know, come from Britain and he, that is, Rudi, comes from a country which, we in Britain call Germany."

"Is that why you seem to get on with each other so well?"

"It is odd that you should say that as, currently, our two nations are at war."

"Then you and Rudi should really be sworn enemies?"

"Paul," said Plum, perplexedly, "I have never been, or ever could be, the enemy of anyone, sworn or otherwise, let alone a person like Rudi. In his amusingly eccentric way he just wants to find his place in the world, enjoy his life and follow his hobby of collecting items for his dressing up box, and ...maybe... trying them on occasionally. I see no hatred or venom in him."

"If you want to see hatred and venom," said Paul, wearily, "try being a Jew, a slave or a farmer, living under Roman occupation – these are, indeed cruel and brutal times."

"I find my fellow human beings to be deeply disappointing at times," said Plum. "Individually they can be quite engaging and capable of great kindness; but then as a nation they periodically develop some kind of collective insanity, which causes them to turn upon each other; blood-letting ensues as their rancour – for whomever their enemy happens to be at the time – grows until they lose all sense of proportion. The killing and destruction then becomes completely mindless and all humanity is subsumed by unbridled hatred."

"Communal Shakespearian foibles?" queried Paul.

"I suppose you could say that," replied Plum, sullenly. "I never thought of it that way but you are probably right."

"Have you noticed," said Paul, "that if you want to motivate people, it seems that the best incentive is to give us something to be against? Ask us to be *for* something and we become apathetic; whereas if you rally us to be *against* something we become instantly invigorated and fiercely resolute."

"Now that you come to mention it," said Plum, "I do recognise that trait in my fellow man but feel powerless when it comes to doing anything about it. It seems that negativity provides a ready bolthole for the lazy. Being positive requires effort."

"It becomes a major problem for me," said Paul, "when spreading the Good News of the significance of Christ crucified and His resurrection and the coming of God's kingdom. I ask those to whom I preach, in a way, to become *for* Christ, by accepting Him into their lives as their path to happiness and eternal life."

"Yes," I'm often mystified by what happened when Christ rode into Jerusalem on an ass and people bestrewed his path with palm fronds; but within days those same people were calling for his crucifixion."

"They were given something to be *against*," explained Paul, "by cries of 'crucify him' from certain people, who had been planted in the crowd by the Sanhedrin."

"And," said Plum, ruefully, "yet again, that simple rally against proved to be effective. What can be done Paul, to alter such obvious shortcomings?"

"Who are we, a couple of flawed human beings, to sit in judgement of others of our kind?" said Paul.

"I will tell you what I think we should do Paul," said Plum optimistically.

"And what would that be Plum?"

"As a good practicing Jew, said Plum, "you will have already read the answer in the Talmud."

"Will I?" enquired a curious Paul.

Plum closed his eyes to aid concentration and began to recite:

And Elijah said to Berokah, 'These two will also share
in the world to come.' Berokah then asked them, 'What is
your occupation? They replied, 'We are merry makers.
When we see a person who is downhearted, we cheer him up.'
These two were among the very select few who would inherit
the Kingdom of Heaven."

"I should have known that the scriptures would provide guidance," said an amused Paul.

"And that guidance is?" Plum asked.

"That we should keep on doing what we do."

"I could not have put it better myself."

"Good night Plum, may God bless you. Sleep well."

"And God bless you too Paul…do you know? I'm certain that he already has."

CHAPTER FIVE

Pads, Pencils and a Picnic

Plum took several notepads and pencils from his typewriter case and handed them round. The assembled cellmates inspected them curiously and muttered amongst themselves about what seemed to them to be really strange objects, especially the pencils.

"What are these coloured sticks for?" enquired Paul.

"They are called pencils and they are used for writing and drawing," said Plum. "If you try them out by placing the pointed tip onto the pad and moving it – the pencil that is – you will see the mark that it leaves."

They all did as instructed and amidst lots of ums, grunts, snorts and tongues-out-of-corners-of-mouths, they began to make lines and curves whilst expressing pleasure and satisfaction.

"When you feel ready, please let me know and I will begin my dictation of the play," said Plum.

Eventually they began to declare that they were able to begin.

"I will, besides telling you what to write," said Plum, "explain where, on your pad you are to place your words. It is important that this positioning of the words be correct as it will make it easier for you to identify your part and learn it."

And so, painstakingly at first and with a few false starts, the dictation and writing progressed. Plum translated from his original English typescript slowly and deliberately as everyone wrote the words carefully in position, before raising their pencils in the air to indicate that they were ready for the next batch. What follows is the play as dictated and translated by Plum, during several sessions over the next six days:

ROSENCRANTZ AND GUILDENSTERN
After Mr W. S. Gilbert, (with apologies)

FIRST TABLEAU

Interior of King Claudius' palace. Claudius discovered seated in a gloomy attitude. Queen Gertrude on a stool at his feet, consoling him.

QUEEN What ails thee my lord!
art thou irked?

CLAUDIUS Irked? My Queen of Queens.
Sad is more the word.

Irked or sad, if by will alone I could

Quash the memory-crowding past — bestrew
The raw-boned and shadowy spectres of outdated deeds,
Or entwine them with lasting cords
In underground chambers imprison,
Then could I, again, smile — but not until then!

QUEEN Oh, my dearest lord!
Whatever it might be that disturbs thy restless soul,
Impart to me that same knowledge.

CLAUDIUS Well, dearest and most faithful wife,
Welcomed rampart to my shambling life,
Yes, I can regale your trustful ear with that that ails me:
Back in my days of mule-headed youth,
I wrote a five-act tragedy.

QUEEN (Intrigued)
Did you, indeed?
A play writ by a nobleman — a true King, no less!

CLAUDIUS A ravening market scooped it up
And, immediately, it was read and accepted.
Then the brotherhood of the scribes of destruction
Wrote of it in their news-bearing rags. Elsinore
Became festooned with placards
Posted by eager hands;
We know that walls have ears — I gave them tongues —
And they were indeed silver-tongues
With pledge and assurance.

The performance drew nearer — all Denmark stood agape.
Provisions were made by which seats might be booked
a full twelve months in advance.
The first night came.

QUEEN And it was a success?

CLAUDIUS In one sense, yes.

QUEEN Oh, I just knew 'twould be so!

CLAUDIUS A farce was given to play the people in —
My tragedy succeeded that. That's all!

QUEEN And how long did it run?

CLAUDIUS About ten minutes.
The first act was barely but part through.
The curtain fell, never to rise again!

QUEEN And did the people hiss?

CLAUDIUS No — worse than that —they laughed.
Sick with the shame that engulfed me,
I sank, palsied, below the parapet of my private box,
And entreated to God that the hearsed and catacombed dead
Might arise and take me for their own!

QUEEN Was it, my lord, so very, very bad?

CLAUDIUS My dear, trusting Queen, it was.

QUEEN And, following this failing of your dramatic offering
Didst though take no steps to rectify thyself in the eyes
of the world?

CLAUDIUS I did.

The acts were five — though by five acts too long,
I wrote an Act by way of epilogue —
An act by which the penalty of death
Was meted out to all who sneered at it.
The play was not good — but the punishment
Of those who laughed at it was capital.

QUEEN My dearest lord, blot it from your mind
And think on't no more. Now hark to me:

To cheer our son, who's forlorn disposition
And tendency to long soliloquy
Have much alarmed us I, without thy knowing,
Have summoned Rosencrantz and Guildenstern —
Two merry knaves, kin to Polonius,
Who will devise such revels in our Court —
Such frolicsome fancies and harmless caprices —
As shall divert his brooding mind
From morose employment.
Claudius, who can tell
But that it might divert my lord's as well?

Enter GUILDENSTERN

QUEEN Ah, they are here!

GUILDENSTERN My homage to the Queen!

Enter ROSENCRANTZ

ROSENCRANTZ (Kneeling) In eager compliance with royal
request.
We have come, good queen, to do our best.

QUEEN Welcome to Court, O purveyors of Royal relief.
Our Chamberlain shall see that you are suitably domiciled.
Here is his daughter. She will heed your wishes
And see that they receive amicable acceptance.

Exuent KING and QUEEN, Lovingly. Enter OPHELIA.

ROSENCRANTZ Ophelia! (Both embrace her)

OPHELIA Rosencrantz and Guildenstern!
This meeting likes me much. We have not met since we were
babies!

ROSENCRANTZ The Queen requested that we come,
And I have embraced this quest in the timid hope
That I, once more, may claim my baby-love!

OPHELIA Alas, I am betrothed!

ROZENCRANTZ Betrothed? To Whom?

OPHELIA To Hamlet!

ROSENCRANTZ Oh, Unbelievable!
Though lovest Hamlet?

OPHELIA (Demurely) That is not what I said —
My words were: 'We were betrothed.'

GUILDENSTERN And what is he like?

OPHELIA He differs from day to day.
Sometimes he's tall — sometimes he's very short —
Now with black hair — now with a thick, red wig —
Sometimes with a German accent — then a Greek,
Then Aramaic with a strong provincial "burr."
Once a Christian, and once a Jew —
But Danish never, take him how you will!
And strange to say, whatever tongue he may speak,
Whether he's dark or fiery red — Greek — Hebrew —
Though he were in Denmark in times that present pass,
He's always dressed as King Herod Antipas!

GUILDENSTERN Oh, he is surely mad!

OPHELIA Well, there again...
Opinion is divided. Some men hold
That he's the sanest, by far, of all sane men —
Some that he's really sane, but shamming mad —
Some that he's really mad, but shamming sane —
Some that he will be mad, some that he was
Some that he couldn't be. But on the whole
(As far as I can make out what they mean)
The favourite theory's somewhat like this:
Hamlet is idiotically sane
With lucid intervals of lunacy.

ROSENCRANTZ We must concoct a plan to stop this match!

GUILDENSTERN Hold hard there! Some time ago, King Claudius
Was guilty of a five-act tragedy.
The play was cursed, and is now mentioned
Only under pain of death.
We might contrive to make Hamlet play this piece before the King,
And take the consequences.

ROZENCRANTZ Impossible! For every copy was destroyed.

OPHELIA But one — my father's!

ROSENCRANTZ Eh?

OPHELIA In his capacity as our Lord Chamberlain*
He has one copy. I this night, when all the court is

drowned in sleep,
Will creep with stealthy foot into his den
And there abstract the precious manuscript!
*(All bow at the mention of this functionary).

GUILDENSTERN The plan is well conceived! But take good heed,
Your father may detect you.

OPHELIA Not so, not so.

My father spends his long official days
In reading all the rubbishing plays.
From ten to four at work he may be found:
And then — my father sleeps exceeding sound!

(Picture. OPHELIA, ROSENCRANTZ, and GUILDENSTERN, grouped.)

ROSENCRANTZ AND GUILDENSTERN

SECOND TABLEAU

Enter QUEEN, meeting ROSENCRANTZ and GUILDENSTERN.

QUEEN How goes your plan to relieve our poor, afflicted,
moping son?

ROSENCRANTZ Madam, the plan goes exceeding well. Already
we have devised some theatricals in which your dear son and
glorious Prince will play a leading part.

QUEEN Ah! That is well reasoned — it will divert his mind. But hush — he comes.

ROSENCRANTZ How melancholy he looks.

Starts — looks around — then, as if reassured,
Rumples his hair and rolls his glassy eyes!

QUEEN (Appalled) Ho! Heaven forefend, that means — he's going to soliloquise!
Stop this, gentlemen, by any means!

GUILDENSTERN We will, but how?

QUEEN Anticipate his points,
And follow out his argument for him;
Thus will you cut the ground from 'neath his feet
And leave him naught to say.

ROSENCRANTZ & GUILDENSTERN We will! We will! (They kneel)

QUEEN A mother's blessing be upon you sirs! (Exit)

ROSENCRANTZ (Both rising) Now, Guildenstern, be on thy metal. Music, Enter HAMLET. He stalks to chair, throws himself into it.

HAMLET To be — or not to be!
Yes, that's the question —

Whether he's bravest who will cut his throat —
Rather than suffer all —

GUILDENSTERN Or suffer all rather than cut his throat?

HAMLET (Annoyed at interruption, says, "Go away — go away," then resumes)
To die — to sleep —

ROSENCRANTZ It's nothing more — Death is but sleep spun out —

(ROSENCRANTZ offers him a dagger).

GUILDENSTERN Why hesitate?

The only question is between the choice of death,
which death to choose.

(GUILDENSTERN offers a noose)

HAMLET (In great terror) Do remove these dreadful things.
They make my blood run cold. Go away — go away!

They turn aside. HAMLET continues.

To sleep, perchance to —

ROSENCRANTZ Dream? That's very true.
I never dream myself.

But Guildenstern dreams all night long — out loud.

GUILDENSTERN (Coming down and kneeling)
With blushes sir, I do confess it true!

HAMLET This question, gentlemen, concerns me not.
(Resumes) For who'd bear the whips and scorns of time —

ROSENCRANTZ (As if guessing a riddle) Who'd bear the
whips and scorns? Now let me see.

GUILDENSTERN (Same business)

Who'd bear them, eh?
Who'd bear the scorns of time?

ROSENCRANTZ (Correcting him) The whips and scorns.

GUILDENSTERN The whips and scorns, of course.

(HAMLET about to protest) GUILDENSTERN continues)

Don't tell us — let us guess — the whips of time?

HAMLET Oh sirs, this interruption likes us not.
I pray you give it up.

ROSENCRANTZ My lord we do
We cannot tell who bears those whips and scorns.

HAMLET (Ignoring them) But that dread something after
death —

ROSENCRANTZ That's true — post mortem and coroner —
Choosing a shroud…where to hold the reception
And then the forfeited life policy —

HAMLET (really furious)
Exceedingly unpleasant. Gentlemen,
It must be patent to the merest dunce
Three persons can't soliloquise at once.

HAMLET retires and throws himself on a dais, as if buried
in soliloquy.

Enter OPHELIA,

OPHELIA (In stage whisper)
Rosencrantz!
ROSENCRANTZ Well?

OPHELIA I've found the manuscript,
But never put me to such work again!

ROSENCRANTZ Why what is it that makes you tremble so?

OPHELIA Last night I stole down from my room alone
And sought my father's den. I entered it!
The clock struck twelve, and then — oh, horrible!

From chest and cabinet there issued forth
The mouldy spectres of five thousand plays,
All dead and gone — and many of them damned!
I shook with horror! They encompassed me,
Chattering forth the scenes and parts of scenes
Which my poor father, wisely, had cut out.
Oh horrible — oh 'twas most horrible! (covering her face).

ROSENCRANTZ What was't they uttered?

OPHELIA I decline to say.

The more I heard the more convinced was I
My father acted most judiciously;
Let that suffice thee.

ROSENCRANTZ Give me, then, the play,
And I will submit it to the Prince.

OPHELIA But stay,
Do not appear to urge him — hold him back,
Or he'll decline to play the piece — I know him.

HAMLET Why what's that? (Rises and comes down).

GUILDENSTERN We have been looking through some dozen plays
To find one suited to our company.
This is, my lord, a five-act tragedy.
'Tis called "Gonzago" — but it will not serve — 'tis very long.

HAMLET Is there a part for me?

OPHELIA There is, my lord, a most important part —
A mad Roman procurator who becomes a Jew
To disconcert the Roman Emperor.

HAMLET That's very good!

ROSENCRANTZ (Turning over the pages) Here you go mad —
and then soliloquise; here you are the same again — and
then you don't;
And then later on, you stab your aunt, because —
Well, I can't tell you why you stab your aunt,
But still — you stab her.

HAMLET That is quite enough.

ROSENCRANTZ Then you become the leader of a troop
Of Greek bandits — and soliloquise —
After a long and undisturbed career
Of murder (tempered by soliloquy)
You see the sin of your ways
And offer to resume your office as procurator;
But it's too late — for, terrible to tell,
As you're repenting (in soliloquy)
The Emperor's guard seize you unawares
And fire you from a ballista!

During this, HAMLET has acted in pantomime the scenes described.

HAMLET (Excitedly) That's excellent.
That is very good indeed — we'll play the piece!

OPHELIA But, pray consider — all the other parts are insignificant.

HAMLET What matter that? We'll play the piece.

ROSENCRANTZ The plot's impossible,
And all that dialogue bombastic stuff.

HAMLET I tell you sir, that we will play this piece.
Bestir yourselves and engage
All the most fairly famed tragedians
To play the small parts — as tragedians should.
A mad Roman procurator! Yes, that is good!

(Picture HAMLET reading the manuscript, with limelight on him. ROSENCRANTZ at entrance, OPHELIA at entrance).

ROSENCRANTZ AND GUILDENSTERN

THIRD TABLEAU

March. Enter procession.
The KING sits, the QUEEN on his left, OPHELIA on his

right, ROSENCRANTZ stands above her, GUILDENSTERN and
POLONIUS behind KING and QUEEN; the COURTIERS right and
left.

QUEEN Good morrow to you, Rosencrantz
How fares the Royal theatricals?

ROSENCRANTZ Limpingly, Madam, limpingly, like a lame
duck.
The Prince has discovered a strange play. He hath called
it, "A Right Reckoning Long Delayed."

CLAUDIUS And what resembles this play?

ROSENCRANTZ 'Tis an excellent poor tragedy, my lord-
A thing of shreds and patches welded into a form that hath mass
Without quality, like an ill-built villa.

QUEEN Why then, sir, did you not steer the Prince's phantasy
Away from such a play?

ROSENCRANTZ Madam, I did, and with some success,
for now he seeth the absurdity of its tragical catastrophes,
and laughs at it as freely as we do. So albeit, the poor
author had hoped to have drawn tears of sympathy, the
Prince has resolved to present it as a piece of pompous
folly intended to excite no loftier emotion than laughter
and surprise. Here comes the Royal tragedian with his troop.

Enter HAMLET and PLAYERS.

HAMLET Good morrow, sir. This is our company of players.
They have come to town to do honour and add completeness
to our revels.

CLAUDIUS Kind sirs, we bid you welcome to Elsinore.
Prepare you now — we are agog to taste
this intellectual treat in store for us.

HAMLET We are ready, sir. But before proceeding
I would address those who are to play this piece.
I have chosen this play in the face of opposition from my
well-esteemed friends. They were for playing a piece with less
bombastic fury and more frolic. (Addresses the KING)
But I have thought this a fit play to be presented by reason of
that very pedantical bombast and windy obtrusive rhetorick that
they do rightly despise. For I hold that there is no such antick
fellow as your bombastical hero who does so earnestly spout forth
his folly as to make his hearers believe that he is unconscious of
all incongruity: whereas, he who doth so mark, label, and under-
score his antick speeches as to show that he is alive to their
absurdity seemeth to utter them under protest, and to take part
with his audience against himself (Turning to players). For which
reason, I pray you, let there be no huge red noses, nor extravagant monstrous wigs, nor course men dressed as women, in this
comi-tragedy; for such things are as much as to say, "I am a comick
fellow — pray you laugh at me, and hold what I say To be cleverly
ridiculous." Such labelling of humour is an impertinence to your

100

audience, for it seemeth to imply that they are unable to recognise a joke unless it be pointed out to them. I pray you avoid it.

Slight applause which HAMLET acknowledges.

FIRST PLAYER Sir, we are beholden to you for your good counsels. But we would urge upon your consideration that we are accomplished players, who have spent many years in learning our profession; and we would venture to suggest that it would better befit your lordship to confine yourself to such matters as your lordship may be likely to understand. We, on our part, may have our own ideas as to the duties of heirs-apparent; but it would ill become us to air them before your lordship, who may be reasonably supposed to understand such matters more perfectly than your very humble servants.

ALL applaud vigorously. HAMLET about to explode in anger, KING interrupts him.

HAMLET thinks better of it and angrily beckons PLAYERS to follow him.

He and they exuent.

CLAUDIUS Come, let us to our places. Assemble with good view
That we might clearly see this fooling. Here's a chair
In which I shall roll about with abandon
When consumed with laughter.
Now we are ready.

Enter on platform loving couple. Applause.

SHE Shouldst thou prove faithless?

HE If I do

Then let the world forget to woo (Kneeling)
The mountaintops bow down in fears,
The midday sun dissolve in tears,
And outraged nature, pale and bent,
Fall prostrate in bewilderment!

All titter through this — break into laughter at the end,
the KING enjoying it more than anyone.

OPHELIA In truth, sir, I hope he will prove faithful,
perchance we should all be involved in this calamity!
CLAUDIUS (Laughing) Much, indeed, depends upon his constancy.
I am sure he hath our prayers, gentlemen!
(To ROSENCRANTZ) Is this play well known?

ROSENCRANTZ (Advancing) It is not, my lord. (Turns back
to OPHELIA).

CLAUDIUS These lines seem, somewhat, familiar. Proceed.

SHE Hark, dost though hear those trumpets and those drums?
Thy hated rival, stern Gonzago, comes!

Exuent loving COUPLE. Laughter, as before.

QUEEN And wherefore cometh Gonzago?

ROSENCRANTZ He cometh here to woo!

Cannot he woo without a lyre player at his elbow? A fico for such wooing, say I!

CLAUDIUS (Alarmed, aside to ROSENCRANTZ) Who is Gonzago?

ROSENCRANTZ He's a mad Roman procurator. Tis a most ridiculous and mirthful character — and the more so for that the poor author had hoped to have appalled you with his tragical end.

ROSENCRANTZ returns to OPHELIA. During this, the KING has shown that he has recognised his tragedy. He is horrified at discovery.

Enter HAMLET as Roman procurator, wearing a toga. All laugh and applaud except the KING, who is miserable.

HAMLET What care I of Rome or State,
I come to wreak my love and hate.
Love whirls me to the lofty skies —
Hate drags me where dark Pluto lies!
All laugh except KING.

QUEEN Marry, but he must have a nice time between them! Oh sir, this passeth the bounds of ridicule, and to think That these times were to have drawn our tears!

OPHELIA Truly, my eyes run down with tears, but they are begotten of laughter!

HAMLET Gently, gently. Spare your ridicule, lest you have none left for later scenes. The tragedy is full of such windy fooling. You shall hear more anon. There are five acts of this!

ALL Groan. HAMLET Resumes.

For two great ends I daily fume —
The altar and the deadly tomb.
How can I live in such a state
And remain with Rome to procurate?

ROSENCRANTZ (Exhausted with laughter) Oh my lord — I pray you end this, or I shall die with laughter!

QUEEN (Ditto) Oh sir, prythee have mercy on us — we have laughed till we can laugh no more!

HAMLET The drollest scene is coming now. Listen.

CLAUDIUS (Rises)

(ALL start)

Stop!

Stop, I say — cast off those mummeries!

Come hither Hamlet!

HAMLET (takes off toga) Why, what ails you, sir?

CLAUDIUS (With Suppressed fury)

Knowst thou who wrote this play?

HAMLET Not I, indeed. Nor do I care to know!

CLAUDIUS I wrote this play — to mention it is death, by Denmark's law!

QUEEN (Kneeling) Oh spare him, for he is my only child!

CLAUDIUS Both shall together perish!

CLAUDIUS drawn dagger. QUEEN endeavours to restrain him.

HAMLET (On his knees) Hold thine hand!

I can't bear death — I'm a philosopher!

CLAUDIUS That's true. But how shall we dispose of him?

ALL puzzled.

OPHELIA (Suddenly) A Thought!

There is a certain isle beyond the sea
Where dwell a cultured race — compared with whom
We are but poor brain-blind barbarians;
'Tis known as Engle-land. Oh send him there!
If half of what I hear of them be true
They will enshrine him on their good hearts,
And men will rise or sink in good esteem
According how they worship him or slight him!

CLAUDIUS Well, we're dull dogs in Denmark. It may be
That we've misjudged him. If such a race there be —
(There may be — I'm not a well-read man)
They're welcome to his philosophic brain —
So, Hamlet, get thee gone and don't come back again!

CLAUDIUS crosses to right, HAMLET, who is delighted at the suggestion, crosses to QUEEN and embraces her. He then embraces OPHELIA, who receives his kiss with marked coldness. Then he turns up onto platform and strikes an attitude, exclaiming, "To Engle-land" At the same time ROSENCRANTZ embraces OPHELIA.

◆

As Plum dictated the last word of the play, the cell door swung open and in swept Prisca, followed by Aquila who, in turn, was followed by a couple of slaves carrying some kind of bier or stretcher on which were stacked a number of wooden containers.

Bringing up the rear, Rudi the guard, in his centurion's uniform, stopped momentarily to take a closer look at the lock on the door which, for some reason, had been proving difficult to operate lately.

"Paul darling," said Prisca, giving him an affecting hug, "I have brought you the things that you requested...and a few additional items which, I'm sure, you and your friends will appreciate." After motioning the slaves to lower their load to the ground, she began delving into the containers.

"Ah yes! Here we have: one lyre." Epaphras stepped forward and took it from her.

"Epaphras is our lyre player," explained Paul.

"Now, where is the other? Ah! here it is: one timbrel." Luke stepped forward. "I take it," continued Prisca, "that you are the timbrel player" Luke nodded.

Useful, unable to restrain himself, was gripping the edge of one of the containers and easing himself up to take a look inside. Aquilla lifted him up so that he could get a closer look.

"Ooh," crooned Useful, "it's full of food and stuff."

"Aquilla and I thought you might like a few treats," said Prisca, "as a change from the food that you are provided within this awful place."

If there was one subject that most occupied the minds of this little band of brothers in their confinement, it was that of food. In their waking hours and in their sleeping hours they thought of little else. The meagre ration supplied by the prison authorities barely sustained them. And so, the main recurring motif in their day...and night dreams was food in all its wonderful guises.

The containers were unloaded and their contents spread around the floor. Plum suggested,

"Shall we put a cloth down and set the food out as if it were on a table? It's an arrangement that, in my home country, we call a picnic."

"I really must bring you some chairs," whined Prisca, alarmed at having to squat on a cold damp and dirty stone floor.

"We must make the best of what we have," said Paul, encouragingly.

Everyone sat around the food-bedecked cloth and began fulfilling their ever-present food fantasies by dipping into the roast chicken, olives, cheese, tomatoes and delightfully crusty bread. The slaves were encouraged to join in – as was Rudi – and so they did with great relish. Plum discovered a particularly gamey cheese, which he spread on his chunk of bread, took a large bite before washing it down with a great gulp of red wine from a gigantic stone jar. There are, he mused, definite perks to this tough prison regime. In fact, he considered popping up to reception to extend his booking for another couple of weeks. 'I am in the Paul Suite,' he would tell them, 'and wish to prolong my stay.' The cheese and wine was, to say the least, 'more-ish' and so he tucked, even further, in.

◆

"What a day of revelry!" exclaimed Plum, as he arranged his bedding...well, his increasingly tatty tweed jacket, before settling for the night. Although some were, by now, snoring, those not already in the land of Nod, registered their agreement by means of 'We agree' type noises.

"Our guard was unusually tolerant in allowing Prisca and Aquilla to stay with us for so long," said a drowsy Paul.

"I feel," suggested Plum. "that Rudi considers himself to be one of the gang now. It is as if he has found a worthwhile direction in life...He has found himself and is able to be who he really is and express himself openly. More of a free spirit, one might say...Well, as far as that is possible for a guard, working for the Roman prison authorities. But there is certainly a fresh spring in his step."

"That is a fine occupation Plum," said Paul... "going around – freeing people's spirits, I mean."

"When we get out of this place," said Plum, chuckling, "we should both beetle round to one of those places where they get you fixed up with a job, and insist that they offer our services as 'Apprentice Going Around Freeing Peoples Spirits Specialists;' or something similar, but maybe a little snappier."

"Like Apostle...or Comedy Writer?" Suggested Paul.

"Paul, what a wordsmith you are – always there with the *mot just*!"

"The what?"

"Oh nothing, it is probably the fault of my Gaul blather. Which reminds me Paul, what sort of cheese was that we had today?"

"It is made from Goats' milk, Plum...very thick and rich."

"Well, it's down in my lower quarters at the moment,

getting pally with the red wine and I think that they are both in party mood."

"You do speak in riddles at times Plum, good night and God bless dear friend."

No answer came there from dear Plum. He was already fast asleep.

CHAPTER SIX

Illusions, Delusions, and a
Struggle for Control

Plum opened his eyes to find that the usually dark, dingy cell now resembled what he imagined the palette of the painter, J.M.W. Turner, might have looked like when that celebrated wielder of the hog's hair brush was engrossed in depicting the last days of *The Fighting Temeraire* or, even more so, *The Angel Standing in the Sun*. The place was suffused in variants of bright yellow, orange and red of the most vibrant hues. The walls, floor and ceiling were not as if painted – the resonant colours appeared to be in the air itself. Over in the corner, someone was playing a piano and Plum thought, on closer inspection, that it might be his dear friend and music composer Jerry Kern, from his days when, together, they had created songs for numerous musical comedies; but the face flickered momentarily and changed to that of Epaphras and then back again to Jerry's. Leaning on the piano and reading, what looked like a script of some kind, was his old friend and colleague, Guy Bolton, whose job it had been to create the book on which each musical comedy would be based. Flicker went the face; oh no, it might be another of Plum's cellmates, Luke, whoops! It's Guy again. There was a woman standing in front of the piano who, he was sure, was Sari Petras, who had played the part of Rosika Wenzel in *Miss Springtime*, a musical that Jerry, Guy and Plum had helped create in 1916. Flicker went the face to reveal that of Prisca; but now, again, Sari! Whoever it was, her song added to the phantasmagoria now pervading the once dark, dank cell, as she sang:

'I've a wondrous castle that I've never lived in yet
Built so many years ago in days that I forget.
It has no stone battlements and
Great big wooden beams.
Its walls and its bars are the dust of the stars.
And its gate the gate of dreams.

Come out there for a visit;
I've lots of room for friends.
And if you ask where it is,
It's where the rainbow ends.

It's somewhere there in Fairyland,
Where there's never cloud or care.
We'll have joy and laughter, mirth and song,
And we'll all be happy as the day is long
In the shelter of my castle
Of my castle in the air.'

In an area in front of the singer, there was a couple dancing to the music. Plum could just make out the familiar figure of Rudi, the guard, dressed as the Queen of Denmark and in the arms of a centurion, who also looked like Rudi. Then, in walked two slaves carrying a stretcher on which teetered, a large cube covered by a deep purple drape with gold edges. The metallic gold reflected the bright Turnerine colours that illuminated the cell? Or was it the Princess Theatre on 39th Street, New York, where Jerry, Guy and Plum had once created their own musical flights of fancy?

The slaves carefully placed the stretcher, with its mysterious load, down upon the stage floor. One of them removed, with a deft flick, the purple cover, to reveal a large transparent tank of liquid. Inside the liquid something was writhing; struggling to free itself from the confinement of the tank and its shackles. A murmur of anguish filled the room – people gasped in horror as, what was now perceived to be a human being struggling in its battle against the finality of death.

After what seemed like an eternity, during which the figure remained completely still, it then righted itself, placed, first one hand on the rim of the tank, slowly followed by the other. Still slowly, but deliberately, it heaved itself up from the depths. Then! With a single leap was standing, free of its chains, in front of the tank. There, raising his hands in triumph stood a beautiful man. Looking extraordinarily like the prison governor, he was in his early thirties, radiated light, even brighter than that of the room, and was wearing nought but a small white cloth about his midriff. His hair was long and, as he smiled radiantly, his white teeth glinted through his youthful beard. Flicker! And in his place stood a cheeky, grinning boy, who shouted, ta dah! It was Useful.

"Plum! Plum! Are you alright?

Plum opened his eyes to find Paul bending over him.

"What is the matter?" enquired a drowsy Plum.

"You were twitching and making peculiar noises," said Paul, "I thought you were in some kind of distress, or maybe having a fit."

"Oh Paul, I had the most bizarre dream. I wouldn't call it a nightmare but it contained the most lurid and strange images. No one seemed to be who they are and everything was so bright – yellows, reds, and so much light!

"But are you alright Plum?" enquired a concerned Paul "you gave me such a fright."

"Well, as alright as anyone could be in the present circumstances," replied Plum, rubbing his head in an attempt to clear it of its recent invaders. "I think, today, if everyone feels ready, we will begin our rehearsals for the show."

◆

Plum had called everyone together and began to speak:

"I think that it is time to begin work on our show and so I have prepared a simple timetable for our rehearsals." He handed Paul a copy and asked that, after studying it, he pass it on so that everyone could read it and, if they felt the need, make comments. This is what he had written:

REHEARSAL PERIODS

Item	Performer(s)	Time allotted
Hymn 1.	Choir	10 minutes
Hymn 2.	Choir	10 minutes
Song of Hybrias the Cretan	Plum	10 minutes
Sonny Boy	Rudi/Useful	20 minutes
Dance Routine	All Dancers	20 minutes
INTERVAL		
Rosencrantz & Guildenstern	Whole cast	60 minutes

"When will this take place?" asked Paul.

"Every day, replied Plum "But I recommend that each item has its own separate period so that whilst that particular item is in rehearsal, all those not involved must refrain from doing anything that might disrupt it. We are all in this one room and total concentration will be necessary if we are to achieve the best results."

"Will we start today Plum?" Queried Luke.

"Yes Luke, if that is all right with Paul, who, as we know, has important work to do.

"I am so interested to see everyone taking part," said Paul, "that I will delay my immediate commitments so that we can begin as soon as possible."

"Hurrah!" Shouted a jubilant Useful, clapping his hands in glee.

"Now," said Plum, "does everyone have a copy of the script for the play?"

"I haven't," said a mortified Useful.

"Yes, you have," said Demas.

"No, I *haven't*," wailed a desperate Useful, fighting back tears.

"Yes, you *have*," Demas repeated, handing him a document, "because I have made you a copy of mine."

"Oh Demas, cried an overwhelmed Useful, taking the script, "is this just for me?"

"Of course, it's for you Useful, it is *your* copy."

"*My* copy," said Useful, gazing proudly at the script. "I've never had anything that was just mine before."

"Well, you have now," said Demas with a twinkle, gently tweaking the young slave-boys nose.

"God bless you Demas," said Paul.

"But I can't read," bawled Useful, "how am I going to learn what I will have to say."

"Well then Useful," said Demas, "you and I will have to work together and I will do the reading for you."

"Aw, would you really, Demas?"

"On that point," said Plum, "the early play rehearsal periods will need to be used for all cast members to work separately on learning their parts."

"Except me and Demas," said a now cocky Useful, "we are going to work together on our parts aren't we Demas?"

"We certainly are," answered Demas, grinning weakly as he began to realise just what he had let himself in for.

As Plum hung the timetable on a hook in the wall, (used on occasions for the shackling of errant prisoners), he announced:

"I will hang this here so that everyone can consult it and, hopefully, bide by the information given."

"Plum," said Paul, "how are we to maintain those very precise time periods when, without word from outside this windowless cell, we don't even know whether it is day or night, let alone the hour or the minute?"

"Do not worry on that score, Paul, I have a gift for such things and will ensure that each period lasts for the time allotted to it." Plum did have a gift and it happened to be the gift of a pocket watch, given to him by his wife, Ethel. When the opportunity arose, he would glance at it surreptitiously, by the lamp on Paul's desk. As the typewriter, and then the pencils, had caused such a stir he had considered it best to keep the watch concealed. He did not want the complication of repeatedly explaining away twentieth century technology; nor did he want to spoil the illusion (or should that be delusion?), seemingly enjoyed by his cellmates, that they are living two thousand years previously.

The twenty minutes spent by the choir on the hymns written by Paul proved to be as beautiful as expected – in fact, it was obvious that everyone knew them so well that the practice session was hardly necessary. Plum then began his rehearsal of Hybrias the Cretan. He had a creditable bass/baritone voice and

117

sang with great gusto. Memories of his happy years at Dulwich College flooded back as he gave vent to the 'Spear Song,' with choreographed arm and body movements that were worthy of the tutelage of their new choreographer, Epaphras. As he finished singing the song (now translated into Greek) for about the fourth time, there came a spontaneous burst of applause from his appreciative cellmates – to which, in response, Plum gave a graceful bow.

It was then time for Rudi and Useful to rehearse their novelty number: Sonny Boy.

"Did anyone show Rudi the timetable?" shouted Plum – "He should be here by now."

"I told him about it, and showed him the timetable" said Useful. "I don't know why he isn't here."

"He is, after all, a prison guard and not a gentleman of leisure, as are we," chuckled Aristarchus, "he might be detained by his duties."

"Never mind," said Plum, "we shall just have to work around it…now let me see, what is up next …"

The door burst open and in walked Rudi, immaculately dressed in a black dinner suit, white dress shirt, black bowtie and black patent leather shoes. From his sleeves shot white cuffs, fixed by gold cufflinks and from the cuffs came dramatic hands covered by expensive white gloves.

"Herr Wodehouse, please forgive me for my late arrival," blurted Rudi, "I had to slip away to put on my costume and so suffered a delay."

"It is so good of you to come at all, Rudi," said Plum, graciously, "bearing in mind your work commitments. But really, this is not a dress rehearsal and there was no need for you go to such trouble."

"But, Herr Wodehouse, for me, the costume is essential if I am to perform to the best of my ability."

"Well, let us get on then," said Plum. "Paul, do you mind if we borrow your chair for a while?"

"Not at all, please do."

Plum placed the chair in the middle of the floor and signalled Rudi to sit upon it.

"Now," said Plum, "Useful, you sit upon Rudi's knee. Rudi, do you know the words to the song or will you, at present, require a written copy?

"No, Herr Wodehouse, I have committed the words to memory."

"Good, said Plum, "then we can proceed. Right, away you go."

Rudi began to sing with great feeling. Useful sat upon his knee – bolt upright and staring into the middle distance.

"Can you stop for a moment, Rudi?" said Plum quietly.

"There's no way of knowing," sang a transported Rudi.

"I say would you mind stopping for a moment? requested Plum.

Rudi ploughed on…"What you mean to me Son…"

"QUIET!" bawled Plum, uncharacteristically.

"Is zer something wrong Herr Plum?" Asked a puzzled Rudi.

"Sorry about my having to raise my voice Rudi," said Plum, "but you were somewhat engrossed and seemed to have difficulty in hearing me."

"Oh, I am so sorry Herr Plum. What is it that you wanted to say?"

"Although your singing is more than satisfactory" explained

Plum, "I think that we need to achieve some affinity between you and Useful. Useful, instead of staring into space, glassy eyed, can you please gaze into Rudi's eyes as if you sense the affection that he transmitting to you... after all, he is supposed to be your loving father...and you, his loving son. Don't you remember the love for, and from, your own real father?"

"No," replied Useful.

"Why is that?" Queried Plum.

"Because I don't know who my father is."

"Oh, my dear Useful, I'm so sorry – how stupid of me to be so tactless."

"That's all right Plum," chimed Useful," I've got Paul, and he loves and looks after me and, thanks to him, I also have the love of Christ Jesus and he will always be there for me, no matter what happens."

"Well said, Useful!" Exclaimed Paul, followed by a general murmur of approbation from the others.

"Well said indeed, Useful," re-joined Plum. "Now let us try the song again but this time with a little more warmth and feeling from the both of you – not that Rudi needs too much more. Away you go"

They went through the whole song – Useful supplying the necessary pathos with the eye and body language. Rudi was word perfect and showed genuine potential as a competent and gifted performer.

"That was a lot better," said Plum, "but, beside the heart-rending emotion, we really need to take some of the seriousness out of the performance by promoting some laughs."

"Laughs Herr Wodehouse?" said a shocked Rudi, "You want

the audience to laugh at my singing?"

"No Rudi, not at your singing, which, by the way, is excellent…"
Rudi beamed, broadly, "…but at the performance," continued
Plum, "which I see as a comedy sketch, let me explain: your serious rendition of the song provides the foundation for the comedy. You sing the words with enormous seriousness and conviction. But, to puncture the pompousness of the ardent emotion
that you, very authentically, create, there must be something
else going on to counter that seriousness…something for comedy impact…but what?"

"I could stick my finger up his nose, chirruped Useful."

"No, you vill not," said an alarmed Rudi, covering his nose
with his gloved hand. "Herr Wodehouse! Tell him he is not to
enter my nose with his finger. Nein, it is verboten! You must not
lay hands on prison staff, on pain of death!"

"O Rudi, do not be so dramatic." said Plum, "The boy is not
going to assault you – he is just offering a suggestion."

"Sorry Herr Wodehouse," said Rudi, regaining his equilibri-
um, "please proceed."

There was a tense silence as Plum sat thinking. Eventually
with a triumphant widening of the eyes and a pointing upward
of the finger, he cried, "I have got it!"

"Got what, Plum? Epaphras asked.

"Whatever it is," chuckled Paul, "I hope it is not
contagious, because I do not want it."

"I once saw a sketch," said Plum "by a very funny comedian
called Sandy Powell. He had a wooden doll on his knee – It was
a ventriloquist's dummy."

"What is one of those?" Demas asked.

"It is a doll," explained Plum, "to which the man directs his voice to achieve the impression that the doll is actually speaking."

"Would not the audience see the man's lips moving and watch him instead of the doll?" Asked Demas.

"To counter that," said Plum, "the man trains himself to speak clearly without moving his lips."

"Wow! exclaimed Useful, "he actually speaks without using his lips?"

"Yes Useful," said Plum. "It is quite common practice in my part of the world. There are many good ventriloquists and some of them make a very good living at it."

Useful's eyes glazed over as he said, "If I really practiced."

Everyone groaned.

"Just stick to your lock picking, Useful." said a wearied Demas.

"Vas ist about der lock picking?" Asked Rudi, narrowing his eyes with suspicion.

"Oh," said Demas hurriedly, "Useful's hobby is collecting locks and he enjoys finding old locks and *picking* them up for his collection."

"There's something about that boy that I find strange," said Rudi, again narrowing his eyes.

"*You* find *me* strange?" Muttered Useful, incredulously.

"Vas ist you say?" Snapped Rudi.

"Range!" spluttered, Useful. "I was just admiring your clothes and thinking what a fine *range* you must have – I wish I had clothes as beautiful as yours."

"Oh, you think so?" said a delighted and, as a consequence, softening Rudi.

"Yes, I am very proud of my collection."

"They always look so good on you," said Useful, relieved that he had averted a potentially difficult situation.

"Sandy Powell," said Plum, "obtained his laughs by purporting to be a ventriloquist but making a complete hash of it. That is not what we want here and so I think we will rely upon the dummy to get the laughs".

"Who's the dummy?" Asked Useful.

"You of course," said Plum.

"I thought I was a doll?"

"And, so you are, Useful."

"It's just that *dummy* makes me sound stupid."

"Not a word," snapped Paul, as Demas opened his mouth to speak.

"I was only going to make a suggestion," said a grinning Demas.

"I know exactly what you were going to say", said Paul.

"I was, if you will only give me the chance," said Demas, with a look of pure innocence, "going to suggest that Useful acts as if he is going to fall off Rudi's knee and that Rudi hangs on to his shirt and struggles throughout, to control him and stop him from doing so."

"You might have something there," said Plum, "but I think that *throughout* might prove too much. I suggest that the struggle takes place between verses, so that Rudi's serious singing performance can be better appreciated."

Rudi preened himself.

"Let us try it that way. Now, Useful, when Rudi reaches the end of a verse, you begin to slide off his knee, or even fall forward.

Rudi, when Useful starts to slide or lean, you yank him back into position, whereupon he begins to, very slowly, slip or lean once more. You can then watch him through the corner of you eye and obtain a few laughs of your own by registering alarm as you drag him back. You regain your composure as you begin to sing but occasionally, whilst singing with great passion, you glance at the dummy – sorry, the *Doll* – with further momentary alarm and a few choice facial expressions. If the audience laughs, go with it. Now, in your own time, off you go."

Not only was Rudi a natural performer; he had an innate gift for comedy. The cellmates roared with laughter at their antics as both Rudi and Useful struggled and gurned with immaculate timing, as they followed Plums instructions.

"Bravo!" Cried Plum as their performance came to a close. "Keep it just like that – especially on the night, and you will slay them."

"Slay them?" enquired a confused Rudi.

"It is an expression used in the English-speaking theatre, replied Plum,

"it means you will have great success with you audience."

"I vish mein Fuhrer knew that – I think he only knows one meaning of the phrase 'Slay them'".

"As do the Roman authorities," said Luke.

"Right," said Plum, "now onto the dance routine. Epaphras I think that, at this stage, I will leave this rehearsal in your hands. And then I will inform you all when the period for practicing our lines for the play is to begin. As already discussed, this is to be done apart and individually at this stage."

"Except for me and Demas," piped Useful.

◆

As Plum was adjusting his pillow (it was his tweed jacket, really) so that one of the buttons did not find its way into his ear, as it had done during the previous night, he said:

"Paul, do you remember when I first came here and you were writing a letter to your church members at Corinth – you know, the one I tried to help you with?"

"Oh, you mean the one with the bits about the Dead sea being only ill and chicken soup and sharks and the like? Plum, how could ever I forget it?"

"Yes, that's the one Paul. Well, at the time you told me about the so-called Jesus movement whose real purpose was to use Jesus as a perfect model of the tradition of Jewish wisdom in their quest to convert the whole world to Judaism; and by so doing, Israel could then preside over a new order of justice and equity throughout the world."

"Yes Plum, why do you ask?"

"Well, it set me to thinking about how such a situation could arise, you know, how did those people develop such an impression of themselves and Judaism?"

"As you know, Plum, I myself am a Jew and proud of that fact. My concerns are not of this earth but for the Kingdom of Heaven. And I, like the majority of my race, do not entertain such self-centred, earthly, ambitions. Never-the-less, to answer your question, I could venture an explanation: It was the Jewish philosopher Philo of Alexandria, who originally preached the 'Jewish Wisdom' tradition. It was influenced by his personal devotion to Sophia, 'Divine Wisdom,' an attribute or emanation

125

of God. This helped give dignity to the Jews who felt humiliated by living under imperial rule.

"There is no doubting Jewish wisdom," said Plum, "it is apparent wherever you look. Do you know? In my part of the world, there is a Jew called Albert Einstein, who, with a piece of chalk and a slab of slate, and by means of mathematical physics, has revealed astounding information on, not only the nature of our world, but of the whole universe. No matter the walk of life, you will find brilliant Jews. For instance, take my area of operations, the musical theatre. My song writing partner, Jerry – or, to give him his correct name, Jerome Kern – a brilliant musician, as is another of my Jewish acquaintances, George Gershwin – and as for Irving Berlin, he can write a popular song – both word and music – that will be on everyone's lips within days of its release to the public. I could go on: theatre managers, set designers, directors, producers – all Jewish and each imbued with pure brilliance."

"Yes," said Paul, "but a reputation for brilliance amongst our numbers does not give us the right to run the world. We can, as you have experienced, contribute, but to use your theatrical parlance, we should not want to run the whole show."

"On thinking about Jews and their, or should I say, 'your', situation in the world. My theory is that, after mankind ceased to be hunter gatherers and began to settle down in one place to farm crops and husband cattle: first hamlets were created, then villages where people lived in close proximity to each other. It was then that – to preserve peaceful coexistence – house rules were required. I suspect that Jewish tribes, when creating such rules, proved to be good at it – so much so that over a protracted period the rules began to grow, not only in number but also in importance until they became law. How many rules are there now, Paul?"

"We call them commandments Plum and there are six hundred and thirteen."

"That, Paul, is a whole lot of experience in rulemaking to put onto the Jewish Curriculum Vitae. And, what a legacy written and agreed rules has provided to mankind for the enabling of collective power. Contracts, treaties, and constitutions now make it possible to enforce agreement between several parties. And should the old foible-peddling individuals raise their disruptive heads, you just tell him, or her, to go and read their copy of the joint agreement. It is not a complete cure for the problem, as my people found recently at a place called Munich, where an odious little man added his signature to an agreement that turned out to be worth less than the paper on which it was written. But, on the whole, the scheme has proved to be a great success.

"But there is something much more impressive Plum that, whilst bringing Jews enormous honour, has brought with it an equally enormous burden of responsibility."

"Ah," interjected Plum, "you mean that God chose, above all others, to speak directly to members of the Jewish race?"

"Yes Plum."

"Oh, that would really bring on a chronic attack of our Shakespearian foibles to the rest of mankind," retorted Plum, "jealousy, envy, covetousness, duplicity – pick where you like, they're all in the same box. Talk about promoting insecurity in others? Being on personal terms with God must be the most effective foible stirrer there could be."

"I am sure that you are right, Plum, but with such a conferment comes great responsibility, and I am not so sure that my people have handled their God-given privilege with the wisdom that they profess."

"Well," said Plum "I suppose that if one goes around reminding people that one of his, or her, kin has been hob knobbing with the Lord himself, it would appear to be a little showy."

"I, as you have probably heard, was once a vehement protector of Judaism, it's traditions and religion," said Paul; but, having been spoken to by Christ Jesus, himself…"

"There you go again," chuckled Plum, "name-dropping."

"No, Plum, hear me out and save the levity for your books and plays."

"Sorry old boy – you know me and my irresistibility to the opportunity of getting a laugh – please, do go on."

"…As I said, having been spoken to by Christ Jesus himself and since studying his ways, I have learned that everyone is equal in the eyes of God. And so, my mission now, is to take the message of knowing and following Jesus as salvation and access to eternal life in the Kingdom of Heaven, to the Gentiles – or, as we collectively call them, Greeks".

"So," said Plum, "anyone who is not Jewish comes into the category: 'Greek."

"Yes, Plum, that is so. I suppose it is because Greek is the commonly used language in commerce throughout the Mediterranean area."

"Unlike the Jesus movement, as mentioned in your letter to the Corinthians – those who wish to preside over the world with their Jewish wisdom – you want the non-Jewish to share with the Jews what God, through his son, Jesus, has promised to all mankind."

"I think that about sums it up Plum," said Paul, yawning. "Now for some refreshing sleep."

"Oh, I do hope," said Plum, "that I have a peaceful night and not one like last night with those vivid images and all those bright red and yellow colours."

"Red and yellow, you say?"

"Yes, that is right Paul, red and yellow."

"Are they not the colours, respectively, of the wine and goat's cheese that you devoured last night?"

"Are you saying that my visions in the night were induced by an over indulgence in red wine and cheese?"

"Could be, could be, Plum."

"I suppose that, coming from someone experienced in the real thing, when it comes to visions, I had better take your word for it, said an impressed Plum."

"Good night and God bless you, dear Plum," said a drowsy Paul.

"Good night and God bless you too, Paul."

CHAPTER SEVEN

The Governor pays a Visit
and Plum takes a Walk

A part from the occasional minor flare-up between Useful and Demas, the studying of the script for the play and the memorising of dialogue, went well. Everyone followed the timetable and all the items were rehearsed as planned. Epaphras had more than proved his potential as a choreographer and the dance routine was looking truly impressive – in fact, there was a good deal of unofficial dance practice occurring as voluntary 'homework' outside the completed rehearsal periods. Some had by now learned the more strident bits of the *Song of Hybrias the Cretan* and, although having been warned off by Plum earlier that it was a solo piece, could not resist joining in with him as he gave it its daily ten-minute airing. Rudi and Useful had everyone convulsed with laughter, as their version of 'Sonny Boy' seemed to produce even more comedy ideas with each performance.

At one rehearsal, Rudi happened to mention that, according to him, his superior approved of the activities going on in this particular cell and that his general feeling was, that whilst prisoners were occupying themselves in such a positive manner, they could not be fermenting trouble. As proof of Rudi's comment, the superior visited the cell during its occupants' rehearsal period. Plum was interested to see that he was dressed in Roman costume and not a German military uniform, also he looked uncannily like the young man who had emerged from the water tank in Plums lurid dream. The superior insisted that, during his visit, they carry on as if he was not there. Plum took the contrary view that having a visitor provided them with a rehearsal advantage. He encouraged them by saying that this was their first opportunity to perform before an audience – even though it was only an audience of one – and that they should take advantage of the experience; and by doing so, they would be better able to perform before an actual audience, should the opportunity present itself.

Every indication was that the 'Prison Governor' (we will call him that, because that is who he seemed to be) was really enjoying himself. He became engrossed in whatever was performed – tapping his feet during the singing and dancing and laughing uncontrollably at the antics of Rudi and Useful. The play was not yet ready and so he was invited to visit again at a later date for a special performance. He gave Rudi permission to take more time off from his prison duties to attend rehearsals, as and when required. After his departure, everyone, including Rudi, became aware of the nervous energy that they had expended in his presence and sank to the floor, exhausted.

"Thank you, all of you," said Plum, "You were magnificent and showed great courage. You performed like seasoned professionals."

As they sat, or lay, recuperating, the silence was broken by Useful,

"Plum,"

"Hullo!"

"You know when you said that we might perform before an actual audience, should the opportunity present itself"

"Yes, my pocket-sized Plato. What thoughts has it stirred in that enquiring mind of yours?"

"Well, we haven't got an audience, have we? It's just us."

"That is very true my precocious, sawn-off Socrates, but, you must admit, that we are better than nothing. At least we can appreciate each other."

"It's not the same though, is it?" said Useful, "It's not like having a real audience."

"Now steady on there young Useful; such talk could have a detrimental effect on the morale of our troupe. It could take the joy out of what we are achieving – you can see for yourself the happiness and extra meaning it has given to our existence."

"I'm sorry Plum, and understand what you say; but, it would be really good to take our show to a proper audience...you know what I mean...lots more people."

"I too wish that that could be so, Useful, but we just have to make the best of what we have got...which, you must admit, is not inconsiderable, when you look at the dear friends that we have around us."

"That's true Plum, they do make life in here a lot easier."

"You possess wisdom beyond your years Useful... by the

way, you're not Jewish, are you?"

"No! Why?"

"Oh nothing…I just thought that maybe Philo of Alexandria had been nibbling at you."

"Who?"

"It doesn't matter. How is your escapology career going?"

"It's coming on."

◆

As Plum hammered away at his novel on the typewriter and Paul busied himself with ink and quill, there came a loud yell from Useful,

"I've done it!" he cried.

"What on earth are you up to now?" enquired an irritated Paul.

"Yes, do keep it down, young Useful," said Plum, "some of us around here are busy preparing to stun the world with our genius."

"But I've actually done it!" exclaimed Useful.

Everyone in the cell turned toward the source of the commotion. Jaws dropped, eyes bulged and those of a more delicate constitution tottered slightly. There, swinging the open door on its hinges stood a triumphant Useful.

"My god!" whispered an incredulous Plum, "He's really done it…he's opened the door!"

"Close it! Close it at once!" hissed Paul.

"But I've only just opened it," wailed Useful.

Paul rushed over and, very gently and quietly, closed the

door. "What are you trying to do Useful," he gasped, "get us all killed?"

"Well you said that if I…"

"Never mind what I said," retorted a very shocked Paul. "If they think that we are trying to escape they will kill us out of hand…*all* of us."

"It was Demas," wailed Useful, "who told me to practice on the lock…"

"Don't drag me into this!" Demas snapped back, whilst taking on the look of a stag at bay.

"But you did! You did!" wailed Useful.

"It was a joke," pleaded Demas, "I didn't think you would actually go and do it."

"Some joke eh, Demas?" taunted Useful, "…You're not laughing now."

"That is enough, you two," said Paul, quietly, "Let us forget the whole thing now and consider ourselves fortunate that the guard did not see or hear anything."

"Don't lock it yet," said Plum to Useful, "I wouldn't mind chancing a walk outside…just to feel the sun on my skin and to smell the fresh air"

"Are you mad?" exclaimed Paul. "If you are caught it will mean instant death."

"Oh, surely not," said Plum.

"Most certainly." insisted Paul, "If they catch you, we will all be blamed and made to pay."

"Then I will tell them," insisted Plum, "that the fault is all mine and that I opened the door and that I am the only one who ventured through it."

"Then you are either very courageous or extremely foolhardy, Plum, I cannot discern which."

"You worry too much Paul," said Plum, as he slipped through the doorway.

◆

Having left the fug of the cell behind, Plum breathed in the fresh, sweet-smelling air. Luckily it was daytime and the sun was bright and warm. He found himself in a spacious yard and, looking back at the door through which he had just come, he noticed that although there were no windows in the cell he had just left, the walls of the building – which was two-storied and in red brick – had a neat row of them for each floor. Looking up he could see faces peering down at him from the upper floor. Surprisingly, they were the faces of some of the men who had made the long train journeys with him from France, first in cattle trucks and for the final stretch – lasting three days and nights – in regular passenger compartments. It was good to see familiar people from around Le Touquet, where he had been living when arrested. There was Algy, from Algy's Bar in the Rue St Jean; Alfred, from Alfred's Bar in the Rue de Paris and William Cartmell, the courteous and popular piano tuner from Étaples. As they eyed him from above, their facial expressions were similar to that of Paul's as he (Plum) had left the cell minutes before. It was as if they, too, expected something awful to happen to him. To allay their fears, he gave them a broad smile and a cheery wave.

Plum strolled around in the sunshine enjoying the sheer

luxury of being in the open air, when across the yard came Rudi.

"Herr Wodehouse!" he called, in surprise. "What are you doing out here?"

"Oh, just getting some fresh air, Rudi. It is so stuffy in there," motioning toward the door with a turn of his head. Rudi showed no sign of distress, as this was 1940 and Plum still remained as an internee within the walls of a former asylum for the insane at Tost in Upper Silesia.

"Would you like a cigarette Herr Wodehouse?" said Rudi, offering an opened packet.

"Oh, that is so kind of you Rudi," said Plum as he took one and placed it between his lips. "I never thought to bring my pipe and tobacco, when, on a whim, I decided to take this constitutional stroll – have you time to join me for a smoke?"

Plum hadn't enjoyed smoking his pipe since he entered the cell. That was because of the panic it might have caused among the occupants, who were not familiar with the exploits of Sir Walter Raleigh's import and export business and his enormous success with tobacco…not to mention the potato. Seeing him setting fire to leaves in a small wooden bowl before sticking it in his mouth, might have proved to people who – because of their already parlous state of mind due to them being imprisoned by a regime noted for its brutality – could easily have proved to be the last straw. The straw, mused Plum, that whilst not actually breaking the back of the poor mammal of the family *Camelidae* (2 species), there was a distinct possibility that it could have occasioned the poor animal to suffer a nasty slipped disk.

Rudi glanced around, saw that the coast was clear and took

out a cigarette. "Yes, Herr Wodehouse, let us sit for a while and enjoy our smoke, together."

"Oh Rudi, I wish that you would drop the *Herr Wodehouse* handle and call me Plum – as do all my friends."

"I am not comfortable speaking to you in such a way Herr Wodehouse; it does not seem respectful. You are a writer of great fame and an English gentleman, it would not be right for me to be so familiar with you in our relationship."

"That is utter nonsense, Rudi," rapped Plum. "As dear Paul says, 'We are all equal' and that, too, is the way I prefer my relationships."

"I'm sorry Herr Plu…Wodehouse, I just cannot do it."

"So be it then Rudi – the last thing I would wish is for you to feel uncomfortable when in my company."

"Thank you, Herr Wodehouse."

"Tell me a little about yourself Rudi…what did you do before the war started? From what I have seen of your theatrical activities in our rehearsals, I would take a wager on you having been in the theatre."

"Then you would win your wager Herr Wodehouse, because that is where I made my living…well, from about the age of seventeen. Originally, I lived in a little village some miles outside Berlin. It was hard, being as I am, to be happy living in a rural community. You see…I could not be myself…I could not express myself fully. And so, at the age of sixteen, I ran away to Berlin in search of an environment in which I could attempt to be who I really am."

"When you said, 'being as I am,'" enquired Plum, "what exactly did you mean?"

"Well, Herr Wodehouse, even to you, whom I have come to trust implicitly," he glanced around to ensure that there was no one within earshot, "it is very difficult for me to explain."

Plum, having been at an all-male public school and spent many years in the theatre, recognised Rudi's furtive behaviour – enforced by the pressure of prevailing social conventions – as that of a homosexual trying to cope with existence in a world of prejudice and ignorance.

"When I got to Berlin about ten years ago," continued Rudi…

"In about 1930?" enquired Plum.

"Yes, Herr Wodehouse, as you say, in about 1930… I began to frequent places where I could find people like myself and after a difficult period, which at times, I'm afraid, involved sin to survive, I obtained a job in a nightclub helping as a dresser…"

"Ah! dresser Dressler eh?" quipped Plum.

Rudi, missing Plum's play on words completely, resumed his potted autobiography:

"Then I began to be given small things to do on stage and progressed from there until I had enough material to do a whole act – or be called upon to take more substantial parts in large and extravagant shows."

"Then," interjected Plum, "that explains your wealth of outfits and your ability to provide your own costumes for our show."

"My collection of costumes started when I was quite young." I knew that I was different, but remained confused as to who I really was. My need for new costumes seemed like a journey on which I might find my true self."

"You see it as your search for an identity?"

"It would seem so," but now I am beginning to think that what it really indicates is that I am like one of those lizard-type reptiles that constantly changes its appearance to suit its surroundings."

"A chameleon?"

"Yes, that is it, Herr Wodehouse, "a chameleon."

"Does being a chameleon bring you any satisfaction?"

"No, it does not."

"Then, what would bring you satisfaction,"

"Just…" said Rudi, with an air of desperation that was almost palpable "…to live in the world and be treated the same as everyone else and not to live each day as one big lie."

"And you are not allowed to do so, confirmed Plum, remembering that the same conditions prevailed in Britain – the derision, the revulsion the use of words like 'queer' 'fairy' and 'Nancy boy.'

"I remember the days when Herr Hitler came to power," said Rudi, "and members of the Nazi S.A. started coming into the club to stand and stare menacingly at me whilst I was on stage – sometimes when I was dressed as a female and trying to perform my act; the recollection of menace in their eyes still causes me to tremble in terror. To make things more difficult for myself with the Nazis, I came under the influence of the local communist party – well, when I say I came under the influence, I saw one of them wearing a most exquisite Russian blouse and thought, Oooh I must have one of those, and so to keep my chic new blouse in context, I could be seen hanging around the offices of the local German Communist Party; the consequence being, more intensive scrutiny from the S.A. and the police."

"What did you do?"

"What I always do to survive,"

"I became a chameleon. First, I left Berlin, went back to my village and presented myself at a nearby recruiting office and became a soldier. The army, with their military uniform, provided the ideal cover. I still live my life as a lie but in the hope that one day I will survive until the time comes when people will learn to see me and my kind for who we really are… people, made by God, to live as every other human being, in peace and freedom."

"Your very own and perfectly true persona,"

"Exactly, Herr Wodehouse."

"I hate to pour cold water on your dream Rudi, but I cannot see it happening in our time."

"But we can live in hope Herr Wodehouse," said Rudi, with an optimistic grin.

They both sat for a time in silence, relishing their cigarettes and blowing the smoke through their lips in a leisurely fashion. When Plum queried:

"Rudi, when you were in Berlin in the early thirties, did you meet any English people?"

"Oh yah…er… yes Herr Wodehouse"

"Can you remember any of their names?"

"Now let me see…there was Chris…now what was his second name?"

"Isherwood?" queried Plum.

"Yah, that was it, Isherwood! Herr Wodehouse, how did you know?"

"I think he mentioned you in one of his books," said Plum, languidly blowing smoke through his nose.

"He mentioned me? Chris mentioned me?"

"I feel certain he did," said Plum…"and he made special mention of your Russian blouse."

"Now you make fun of me, Herr Wodehouse."

"No Rudi," I would never laugh at you, unless of course you wished it…say, for instance, when you clown – as with Useful in our show. After we get through this dreadful conflict, try to obtain a copy of his novel, which, if I remember correctly, is called, *The Berlin Stories*. In fact, you are again mentioned in that same book …I think I recollect…in the penultimate paragraph. Isherwood expresses his concern for your safety. He says something like:

> *'The Nazis won't laugh at him; they'll take him on trust for what he pretended to be. Perhaps at this very moment Rudi is being tortured to death.'"*

"Then," said Rudi, proudly, "Herr Isherwood has underestimated Rudi Dressler, the Chameleon of the Kleiststrasse,"

They sat quietly for a while, watching the smoke from their cigarettes as it drifted until dispersed in the warm air. Eventually, Rudi broke the silence:

"Herr Wodehouse, what did Herr Isherwood write about my Russian blouse? Did he say that it looked stylish?"

"Not quite Rudi, not quite. Find that novel and discover for yourself what he actually wrote."

"And now," said Plum, stubbing out his cigarette, rising and stretching himself, "I had better get back to my cell before Paul frets himself into an early grave, at my absence."

"You do not need to go back Herr Wodehouse, you could, if you wish, go and join the other internees, including the ones who travelled with you from your home town, in France."

"Much as I miss my fellow travellers, Rudi," I have developed a powerful affinity with my cellmates in the windowless, rock box and feel that I must return to them. After all, I have grown very fond of each of them and feel that I have an obligation to them…we have our show to perform…and that leaves a lot of joy to be shared."

Wondering at the fact that Rudi had not asked him how he had gained his brief freedom, Plum slipped back in through the cell door. The relief at his return was, for Plum, extreme-ly touching. On seeing him emerge, silhouetted against the dazzling light that flooded in through the sun-drenched portal, Paul beamed so widely that his face was in danger of splitting like a freshly boiled egg, under the spoon.

"My dear, dear Plum, we are so pleased to see that you have returned. We truly feared for your life."

"Well, my dear Paul, here I am as large as life and twice as handsome – thanks to my brief sojourn in the sun I now possess the visage of a bronzed, Greek god…well almost."

Useful rushed forward and threw his arms around what should have been Plums waist but, owing to their difference in height, ended by corralling a couple of femurs some two feet lower down.

"Oh Plum, Plum," sobbed Useful, burying his face in Plums voluminous tweed plus-fours, "I thought I'd killed you with my stupid fiddling with that lock."

"Please do not fret so, my pint-sized paladin. You demonstrated enormous persistence and determination and deserve nought but the highest praise. Against all those who doubted your ability to achieve the goal you set for yourself, you prevailed with aplomb. If their estimation of you has not risen immensely, following your amazing exposition of self-belief-in-action, then the problem is all theirs. In my eyes, you contain the stuff from which heroes are made."

"Do you really think so Plum?" said Useful emerging, tentatively, from the fulsome Harris Tweed.

"My dear Useful," Plum reassured, "I do not just *think* so; I am indeed, *sure* so...by the way, how did you manage it – opening the door I mean?"

"With a rusty nail, I pulled from one of the boxes that Prisca and Aquila brought," said Useful, carelessly – regaining his briefly lost confidence. "I just stuck it in the keyhole and kept wiggling it about until, ta da! It opened."

"A rusty nail eh?" said an impressed Plum. "So, you applied some tried and tested technology, did you? You say that you just kept wiggling it about? ...You are sure that it was a wiggle and not a waggle?"

"What's the difference?" queried Useful.

"I am not sure," whispered Plum, conspiratorially, and with a grin and a twinkle of the eye, "but I am certain that there must be one."

Useful saw that Plum was pulling his leg and began to laugh. Seizing the moment Plum added:

"That Noah chap must have been a firm believer in nails, rusty or otherwise, because he certainly knew what he was doing when he secured his forty cubits with them…but, I wonder… was that *before* the Iron Age? If so, he probably used wooden pegs."

"Wooded pegs to open a lock?" queried a grinning Useful – turning the table on Plum and gaining the upper hand as leg-puller.

"No, to…oh it doesn't matter," said Plum, smiling as he headed back to his typewriter, safe in the knowledge that his young cellmate had now been restored to his previous optimistic and ebullient self.

◆

"Do you know, Paul?" said Plum, arranging his suitcase and jacket to resemble, what he considered, might effect an improvement to his once, 'jacket-only' pillow, "existing as we do in this cell, reminds me of life in general."

"In what way, Plum?" enquired Paul.

"Well, we entered this room," explained Plum, "just as we did when we entered life…and, eventually, we will leave life just as we will leave this room. We exist in this room as we exist in life, by creating things to do; activities with which to fill in our time while we wait for release."

"That is a very bleak outlook, Plum," replied Paul. "But you are right about waiting, and never more so than at present, as we await Christ's imminent return."

"It is not that I am complaining about filling in my time," said Plum, "in fact I love what I do and would be quite satisfied to keep on doing it for all eternity."

"Then your situation is extremely rare, because, as you must have realised, there are very many others trapped by circumstance into a life of hardship and misery. You are blessed with creative skills and the ability to employ them to best effect and, consequently, to gain material comforts."

"That is true, and I never, for a moment, take my good fortune for granted. I have setbacks and disappointments, as does everyone, but on the whole, would not change a thing."

"The real reason for *living*, and not just existing, is Christ," said Paul; "He came at a time when we really needed him. Life under Roman occupation is very hard indeed, making it difficult; not only for Jews but for everyone outside of the ruling classes to retain their dignity and self-respect. Jesus provided a release from oppression. He is someone we can really trust and believe in, someone who will always be there for us – someone whose sole purpose – not just in our earthly life, but also in the life to come – is to teach the way of love and peace – the perfect antidote to the worldly way of, conquer by force, then peace for a while before yet more conquering by force. In the kingdom that Christ promises, everyone is valued and treated equally... Plum, do you see that solitary oil lamp on my table...how its flame illuminates this dark place? Well that is exactly what Christ's presence in the world has done for mankind. Can you imagine what existence would be like living in this stone box – or, for that matter, outside it – without the light of the world...for that is what Christ Jesus is; He is truly *The Light of the World*. We do not enter and leave an empty box, as you suggest but, through faith, live in the light, and with purpose.

So now, to help us survive, we have appropriated the phrases as used by our occupiers when displaying their loyalty to the Emperor. We now use those same phrases for the worship of Christ Jesus. To the followers of Christ, such phrases are only appropriate when used to describe someone whose purity of purpose has truly warranted them."

"Can you give me some examples of those phrases, Paul?" I really would appreciate the opportunity to learn some of them. It will help me recognise them for what they really mean when they crop up in conversation."

"Certainly," Now, take the phrase, *The Good News*, which, as you must know by now, means the good news of the coming of Christ, who through his ultimate sacrifice on the cross, has liberated mankind from its sins. That particular phrase is used on Roman coins and inscriptions to announce that Emperor Augustus, the 'saviour' had established an era of peace throughout the world. The fact that he had achieved it by means of sustained cruelty and violence is not mentioned. We often refer to our Lord Jesus as the, *Saviour of the World*, a title assumed previously by the Emperor Claudius."

"I see," said Plum. "That means that you can talk freely about Christ by using phrases common to all those around you – including those of the authorities – without attracting suspicion."

"Yes Plum, to be heard praising anyone above the Emperor is a serious offence, punishable by death. As the phrases we use, when praising Christ, appear on the coins in their purses and on official proclamations, they have become very familiar indeed, leading them to believe that we are talking about their beloved Emperor. But we know who we are really taking about."

"You could say," quipped Plum, "that the phrases are common currency...."

"Literally, Plum."

"...To coin a phrase," added Plum.

"Mr Wodehouse," chuckled Paul, "you are incorrigible"

"You are right there Paul, you cannot corridge me...good night and God bless you."

"And may God bless you, too, Plum. Good night and sleep well, my dear friend."

CHAPTER EIGHT

Small Kindnesses, Grand Gestures
and Freedom Unrecognised

The play, *Rosencrantz and Guildenstern*, which had been in rehearsal for many weeks, had now reached a stage when it was ready for public performance. With Plumb's permission, Rudi had informed the prison governor of the situation, telling him that the cast were ready to perform the play for him whenever he found it convenient to attend. That day had now arrived, as had the governor. He settled himself in Pauls chair.

"Well gentlemen," he said, "you may proceed when ready."

At Plum's signal, the actors involved in the opening scene made their entrance from a dark corner of the cell into an area illuminated by the solitary lamp on Paul's table, and the play began. The cast, riding on a tide of adrenalin, performed very well indeed and grew in confidence with each succeeding scene. The governor sat outside the pool of light and could not be seen. Not that it mattered, as the actors were concentrating so intensely that they would not have seen him anyway. It was only as the final scene came to an end and the cast made its final bow that they suddenly remembered his presence.

They stood in the dark corner, to which they had made their exit, and waited. Silence prevailed for, what seemed like an age.

Into the lamplight stepped the governor, sullen faced. Oh dear, thought Plum, he has not understood it...he has missed the humour...especially the part involving the Roman procurator...I have done it now...brought trouble on my dear friends. Plum was just about to blurt out that it was all his idea and that no blame must be attributed to the others, when the governor's face broke into a wide smile and he began to clap his hands and exclaim:

"Bravo! Bravo! Bravo! That was wonderful, wonderful."

"We are so pleased that you enjoyed it," said Plum, almost in a state of collapse from relief.

"Enjoyed it? Enjoyed it?" bellowed the governor; "more than that...I *loved* it! In fact, I want others to see, enjoy and love it too."

"See," said Useful, buoyed by the relief of not having to be slain for insulting the Empire, "See Plum, we might get our real audience after all... one with lots of people"

"Leave that to me," said the governor, "and I will see what I can do."

"Would that be just for the play or the whole show?" enquired Plum.

"I have now seen all of it," said the governor, "and enjoyed all of it and for me it has to be the whole show."

"Hurrah!" shouted the cellmates, as spontaneous hugging, back- slapping and vigorous hand shaking broke out among them.

"What I first saw in this cell caused me laughter, melancholy and a whole gamut of other emotions. What I have seen today has had a similar effect," said the joy-filled governor. "The whole experience has lifted my spirits."

"That being the case," said Plum, "we have achieved what we set out to do, and I am sure that I speak for the others when I say that, we are delighted."

"It was what you were put on this earth for Plum," said Paul, with just a hint of a tear on his right cheek.

"Compared with the joy inspirited by you, Paul," said Plum, "I am merely a performing flea in the tiniest of circuses."

Paul, realising the danger, should the governor construe Plum's words as referring to his promoting the Christian way (the very reason for his incarceration), answered,

"Oh Plum, you mean *The Good News* of the *Saviour*, who has established an era of peace throughout the world?"

"Ah! You mean the Emperor Augustus?" said the governor, with a wry smile.

The cellmates, recognising that there was hoodwinking in progress, nodded their heads enthusiastically and beamed, broadly.

◆

"Paul, I am certain," said Plum, as they sat quietly recovering from the governor's recent visit, "that it is the small kindnesses exchanged between human beings that have the most profound and lasting effects. Grand gestures are all very well, but the pitter-patter of regular kindness and benevolence is like spring rain to the burgeoning flora. We were all terrified about getting it wrong in the presence of the governor – and the dire consequences had we done so – when his face blossomed into a smile and the world became, once more, a happier place."

"Do you not think?" replied Paul, "that, in that situation, the slightest twitch of the corners of his mouth in an upward direction constituted a grand gesture?"

"Well, I suppose that the seriousness of the situation made it so…but you know what I mean. Let me give you an example from personal experience:

"It occurred when I was being transported to this place in a wagon, with around fifty other men; we waited for eight hours for the truck to start moving – standing all the time, as there were too many of us in the confined space to be able to sit down – it was then that dear Bert Haskins, whom I had met in camp, suddenly appeared at my side with half a loaf of bread, butter, radishes, a bottle of wine and a slab of potted meat. He didn't know me but, out of the sheer goodness of his heart, he came and gave me the stuff. I had read of a similar occurrence in a fine book called War and Peace, in which one of its main protagonists had been captured by the enemy and imprisoned, during a battle. Just as Bert Haskins did for me, so did an illiterate peasant…I think he was called Platon Karataev…did for his fellow prisoner, an aristocrat…who, I'm certain was called Pierre Bezuhov. As Pierre sat in the shed in which they were being held as prisoners of war, Platon, the simple but stoically, ever-happy peasant, unwrapped some baked potatoes from a bit of cloth, and passed them to him. Then, taking out a clasp knife and another bit of cloth containing salt, went on to instruct Pierre on how best they should be eaten. Leo Tolstoy confirmed my case precisely, when he wrote,

'There is no greatness where simplicity, goodness and truth are absent.'

I do not know," continued Plum, "whether, like me, Tolstoy had had a real-life experience of meeting someone like Platon Karataev, but he was obviously aware that it is quite possible to run into a saint in the most unexpected of places.

"This person…" ventured a quietly impressed Paul.

"Platon Karataev?" interjected Plum.

"No… Tol somebody. The writer"

"Oh, Leo Tolstoy" replied Plum.

"Yes, Leo Tolstoy," said Paul, "He possess the same qualities as your William Shakespeare – great insight, empathy and innate wisdom."

Plum was tempted to say, 'the same legacy of Christian teaching,' but resisted from doing so.

Useful, who had been listening silently and, it might appear, reading Plum's thoughts, jettisoned his uncustomary repose with the words, "You couldn't very well say that Jesus' dying on the cross to remove our sins and bring us eternal life was a small kindness. That must be as great a kindness as you will get in an eternity of lifetimes."

"You are right, Useful, to make such an observation," said Paul. "But that eternity of lifetimes, as you call them, must be lived – particularly the ones here on earth and, surely, it is the small day-to-day acts of kindness to each other that bring constant joy?"

"Let us face it, Useful," said Plum, grinning, "We cannot top Jesus, when it comes to grand gestures, kindness or anything, for that matter, and so we will stick to what we can manage…you know, just chipping away with the small but precious stuff."

"Sounds good to me Plum," replied a grinning Useful.

The voice of Epaphras rose in song:

We will be kind to the stranger.
For we lived as strangers in the land of Egypt.
We are filled with pity now!

We will be kind to the widow.
For we lived as strangers in the land of Egypt.
We are filled with pity now!

If they cry out, if they cry out, if they cry out
We will listen.
For we are filled with pity now!

We will be kind to the orphan.
For we lived as strangers in the land of Egypt.
We are filled with pity now!

We will be kind to the poor man.
For we lived as strangers in the land of Egypt.
We are filled with pity now!

If they cry out, if they cry out, if they cry out
We will listen.
We are filled with pity now!

After the first line, the others joined Epaphras in a call and response style, with him singing, 'We will be kind,' etcetera for each verse, and all the others replying with, 'For we lived,' etcetera. Everyone sang together on the chorus, 'If they cry out...'

"What compelling words." Commented Plum. It is as if all that is civilised about the human race is encapsulated in those few stanzas.

Where did you find that song Epaphras?"

"The words – in this instance, paraphrased – are to be found in the Talmud – in Exodus. The melody? I don't know where that came from...I just picked it up from somewhere."

"A few years ago, back in my part of the world," said Plum, "we had a dreadful war, which has now been followed by a second. Great upheaval was caused, which meant that, in both conflagrations, many millions of refugees had to flee the war zones for their own safety or by suffering forcible deportation by the state in which they lived. Some people came to their aid – even small communities rallied together to provide food and accommodation – bearing out the qualities of humanity as contained in your song."

"Small kindnesses Plum, small kindnesses. "said Paul.

"I am afraid, Paul, that, disappointingly, there were some unfortunate Shakespearean foibles to follow. After a while, certain members of those same communities turned against the refugees in their midst, claiming that they did not show enough gratitude for the help that they were given. What price real altruism? It would appear that with some people, kindness and charity have a limited time span, after which the rosy glow, provided by their philanthropic adventure, pales and they return to thoughts of self-interest. Some people were so extreme as to want to keep all refugees and asylum seekers outside their country's borders. There are always, of course, those who remain dedicated to the welfare of others. If, as you say, the words of your song come from the Talmud, then that means they were written down around one thousand four hundred years ago (three thousand four hundred for me, thought Plum); and still not all of us have taken them fully to heart.

"Then Plum," said Paul "we will just have to work harder until they do."

◆

The cellmates had enjoyed several hours of peace and quiet, some of them snoozing, to recover from the rigours of their recent performance before the governor, when the cell door opened and in came Prisca and Aquila, followed by Rudi.

"My dear Paul, and friends in Christ," trilled Prisca, "How are you all? Well, we trust?"

"Considering", said Paul, smiling, "that we barely subsist on a meagre prison diet – somewhat limited in its variety – have not, except for Plum, seen any sunshine for so many months that we have lost count, and sleep on a stone floor, we are, if nothing else, in good spirits."

"Oh! I'm so sorry," said Prisca. "Do forgive my thoughtlessness…it is just my way of trying to bring you some cheer and to brighten your day."

"A small kindness?" enquired Useful with a twinkle.

"Yes, exactly, Useful, A small kindness," said Prisca.

"And we appreciate your small, but welcomed, gesture" said Paul, "it is always a pleasure to see you both. Is this just a social visit, or have you brought news?"

"Well, we came," said Aquila, "to see if there is any truth in a rumour that is circulating in the city"

"Rumour?" enquired Paul, "What rumour?"

"That the followers of The Way, imprisoned in a cell at this particular establishment are going to perform in an entertainment and that it is to take place at the amphitheatre."

"The amphitheatre?" came the cry from all the cellmates.

"The amphitheatre?" asked an incredulous Paul, "Where did you hear that?"

"Everywhere," cried an excited Prisca. "Everyone is talking about it – it has caused quite a stir!"

"Let me explain," interjected Rudi, "I meant to tell you all but have been so busy with my duties that I could not find the time to get here."

"Tell us what?" enquired Plum.

"It appears," said Rudi, "that the governor left here and immediately ordered one of his staff to go straight to the amphitheatre with a note requesting the hire of the building for a special performance. He has now arranged for us to actually perform our whole show in the amphitheatre."

"Christians…in that large round part in the centre the… large open space with no seating but lots of sand?" queried a puzzled Plum.

"Yes, I think it is called 'the Arena,'" said Rudi. "That is where we are to perform…and I don't' know about you, but I can't wait."

"Christians…in that large open part with lots of sand, which I'm told makes it easier for soaking up blood for easy removal? That part?"

"Yes, that part, Plum," replied Rudi, "Why are you so concerned?"

"He…the governor that is…" continued Plum, "did he mention anything about adding lions…and maybe, the odd tiger to the cast…just to give the show an extra bit of zip for the amphitheatre regulars?"

"Oh, I see what you mean," said, a now querulous Rudi, "You don't think that we are to be the butt of some tasteless, Roman ruling class, joke?"

"Like," ventured Plum, "Come and see the Thespians versus Felines Show of the Year, as a bunch of Christians attempt to act their way around the prides of Africa and Asia – led by Leo and Stripy! As you say Rudi, 'I can't wait.'"

"Surely, Plum, you exaggerate," said Paul, calmly. "It was plain to see that the governor was sincere in his enjoyment of our show, and very enthusiastic to have us take it to a larger audience."

"Well," said a philosophical Luke, "regardless of whether it is to be a genuine performance or a sadistic joke, there will be little, if nothing, that we can do about it, and so we had better just go along with it."

"It will give a whole new impetus to what we in Britain call 'First night nerves,'" said Plum. "That is for sure."

"I can't understand it," said Demas, the governor has not been gone for very long and now all this is happening – what has caused all the excitement – and so quickly? It is not as if a troupe of well-known and popular actors is visiting the city… it is just us, a small group of unkempt prisoners…and not even professional performers at that!"

"I am a professional!" snapped an offended Rudi.

"What is it," continued Demas, "that has everyone in such a state?"

"That was the other thing that I came to tell you" said Prisca. "It is because Alexander the coppersmith, on hearing that the event is to feature followers of The Way, has been rallying everyone to a demonstration that he is planning to take place outside the amphitheatre."

"That will please the regulars." said Plum, "From what I know of them, they appreciate some argy bargy… with maybe just a soupçon of blood-spilling for good measure."

"Alexander the coppersmith has already done me a lot of harm," Paul moaned, "He has been bitterly contesting everything that we say. We had the same problem at Ephesus with a silversmith called Demetrius, who employs a lot of craftsmen making silver shrines of Artemis. They, of course, derive their livelihood from making and selling effigies of that, so-called goddess. And so, when I declared that gods made by hand are not gods at all, my speech roused them all to fury and they started to shout, 'Great is Artemis of the Ephesians!' which they kept up for hours. I really do not want a similar situation to arise at the amphitheatre. Things became very ugly and dangerous…and if they do in this case, and if the governor is blamed for allowing it to happen, he will be punished severely and his successor will take extreme measures to ensure that his prison holds no one who can bring him to the attention of the Imperial authorities."

"If there is anything that Roman regional rulers do not like, it is unrest of any kind," said Luke. "They like to be seen as a safe pair of hands and their standing in Rome depends upon them keeping the peace within their region, at any cost. If we are going to survive, should an incident arise at the amphitheatre, we must be seen to be no part of it and keep our heads down."

"Should an incident arise," said a concerned Paul, "it will be too late by then and our fate will be sealed."

"So much for our show and our real audience," groaned Useful. "I knew something would have to spoil it."

"Maybe if the governor hears about the demonstration planned for the amphitheatre, he might call the whole thing off," said Plum, brightening.

"We will just have to wait and see," said Paul.

"And hope for the best," said a despondent Aristarchus.

"After all, it is only a show." ventured Demas, "Staying alive is much more important."

"I know," said Plum, resignedly, "but it is such a good show."

◆

Rudi reported, surprisingly, that the governor had not adopted the strategy of calling the whole thing off but seemed even more resolved to have the performance take place.

"Does that mean," queried Plum, "that demonstrating – by the conduct of his well-behaved inmates – the orderly running of his prison is more important to him than risking a baying mob outside the amphitheatre? And how do we know that he is not going to placate the unruly assembly by serving us up as canapés for Leo and Stripy and their ravenous pals?"

"As I have said before, Plum," said Luke, "we do not know, and there is absolutely nothing that we can do about it."

"Luke," Plum enquired, "have you ever considered changing your name to Job?" You little ray of sunshine."

"You're a fine one to talk Plum," re-joined Luke, "with your constant mention of lions and tigers."

"It is only my way of trying to lighten the proceedings, Luke," said Plum. "You know that I am only joking."

"I do not find it funny" answered a perplexed Luke.

"Well!" piped Useful, "If we are to be used, as Plum says, to feed the cats, let us give our audience something to remember us by. We can give them a performance that they will never forget."

"And", said Paul, "show them that, with our faith in Christ Jesus, we remain justified and unafraid."

"Aye!" cried the cellmates, to a man, raising their fists in the air.

Plum, though not the fist-raising kind, got caught up in the moment and joined in. "Once more into the rehearsals dear friends!" he cried, and mumbled something about, "On this Saint Crispin's day."

"Whose Saint Crispin?" queried Useful, "Is he one of the Corinthian or Thessalonian lot?"

"No," replied Plum, "it's just someone whom William Shakespeare mentioned in one of his plays…it was in one of his rousing speeches…it just seemed appropriate. Well come on everyone, let us polish that show!"

Following a rigorous rehearsal, Plum asked Rudi, discreetly, if the door might be left unlocked so that he might take a stroll and enjoy a smoke, outside.

"I will divulge to you a little secret, Herr Wodehouse," whispered Rudi, as he was leaving the cell, "The door has never been locked."

◆

A little later, Plum had tried the door and, as Rudi had indicated, found it to be unlocked. He had opened it quietly, just enough to squeeze through to make his temporary escape. Strolling over to the low wall in the yard to take a seat, he was not surprised to see Rudi already there, sitting quietly and dragging on a cigarette.

"Rudi," said Plum, "what is this about the door remaining permanently unlocked?"

"I don't know why it remains unlocked Herr Wodehouse; it's just that it has a key that is completely ineffectual. To give the impression that I am the guard of this area of the prison, I make a show of unlocking and locking the door as I come and go. That place is a haven to me; the people in there are so kind and non-judgemental that it provides the only place where I can feel contented and at peace with myself…If only we could multiply the kind of people in that cell until they filled the whole world…what a wonderfully, warm, co-operative and joyful place it would be."

"That was what Paul and his Christian friends were attempting to do when they started out teaching The Way, two millennia ago," said Plum. "Although I do not think they realised it at the time. Paul thought and consequently, so did his followers, that Christ would return in their lifetime and put the world to rights. But, what it seems they were actually doing was Christ's work, not so much in his absence, but through his spiritual presence in them. I suppose you could say through the power of their faith. Christ had laid the ground with his teaching during his physical presence and now they were keeping his teaching alive until his return. His return though, is taking longer than they thought and in the meantime what they began has now encircled the world."

"Yes, Herr Wodehouse, the fact that the message preached by, what seemed like, a simple son of a carpenter from a tiny hamlet in an area of, at that time no great importance in the world, has resonated so profoundly and for so long that it *has* to have a special significance. It seems to have had the same effect as water to the parched."

"And bread to the starving," agreed Plum. "What is it, do you think," continued Plum, "that keeps our dear friends from trying to escape? Why have they not discovered that they are not locked in? And what about visits from the governor…is he really a Roman prison governor…or someone, or something else? Is he of their time or of ours?"

"Is it a mystery to you, Herr Wodehouse?" Rudi asked,

"Yes, is it not to you Rudi? And there is another aspect I also find to be strange: that being, a Roman prison governor who displays kindness and concern for his prisoners. From my limited knowledge of prisons in the period of the Roman Empire, they were very cruel and brutal places. Prisoners remained in shackles during the whole of their confinement. I know that our friends suffer extreme hardship in there, but at least they can move around within the cell."

"Yes, Herr Wodehouse; I can understand that it must unsettle you.

"Does it not you Rudi?"

Rudi remained silent.

"And, there is another thing," said Plum, "why is the governor ignoring the potential danger of allowing banned Christian prisoners to parade themselves in a very public place? It all seems very mysterious and strange to me."

"I can appreciate that Herr Wodehouse."

"Since the minute that I walked through that cell door," remarked Plum, "'mysterious and strange,' would seem to sum up the whole experience. Not that I am complaining. It is, after all, a very enlightening, heartening and, for all its discomforts, joyful experience."

"That is true, Herr Wodehouse, one cannot help but feel that one has been given the privilege of witnessing something very important in the affairs of mankind as a whole."

"When I first came here Rudi, I thought that all the others in my cell were mentally deranged. I had been informed that this building had previously been an asylum for the insane and concluded that my cellmates were the last of the inmates, still awaiting transport to another place."

"I can fully understand why you would think that way, Herr Wodehouse."

"But now after spending time with them – and I realise that this might sound as insane as I thought they were – I am convinced that they really are some of the original early Christians, as recorded in the new testament of the bible. How they came to be here I do not know; but they are here and you and I, I am sure you will agree, are enjoying the company of some – though simple in their demeanour – very special, powerful, and influential people, indeed."

"Not powerful in a sinister way, Herr Wodehouse, as is often the case with people attracted to power."

"You mean like Adolph, your Fuhrer?" joked Plum.

"No, no, no," blustered Rudi, in triplicate as he always did when perturbed or excited. He then peered around to check that no one could hear him, before whispering: "Yes, Herr Wodehouse, like Herr Hitler."

Plum whispered back, conspiratorially, "Yes Rudi, I think Adolph has cornered the market in 'Sinister.'"

Rudi covered his mouth with his hand, but his bobbing shoulders betrayed the truth that Plum's remark (assisted by special twinkle) had tickled his funny bone. Plum, enjoying the moment, decided to catch him on the crest, as it were, by rehearsing a conversation that took place in the bar-parlour of the Anglers' Rest, in one of his short stories, *Buried Treasure*.

Becoming quite serious, Plum cleared his throat and addressed Rudi with the words:

"In my opinion, Rudi, Hitler is standing at a crossroads and will soon be compelled to do something definite."

Rudi, wide-eyed, focused upon Plum and awaited the further deliberations of this distinguished, English gentleman.

"His present policy," continued Plum, "is mere shilly-shallying. He'll have to grow it or shave it off…He can't go on sitting on the fence like this. Either a man has a moustache or he has not. There can be no middle course."

For a moment, Rudi remained stunned, as his uncertain mind considered further what Plum had said. Silently, he mouthed the words to himself "...Either a man has..." Then the pfenig dropped and he began to laugh uncontrollably – so much so that Plum had to grab him as he teetered backward and was in danger of falling off the wall, on which they were both sitting. Rudi's unbridled laughter became contagious and so Plum, too, began, at first to chortle and then, like Rudi, lose complete control and rock with laughter.

Wiping the joyful tears from his eyes, Plum, pulling himself together as best he could, said, "Rudi, whatever you do, do not tell Useful about the door being permanently open. After his dogged effort whilst picking the lock.

"Ah!" interrupted Rudi, "So that story about him picking up locks to put in his collection was complete nonsense."

"I am afraid so Rudi. You see, we thought that you really were our prison guard and that, should we escape, you were afraid of suffering the consequences. But now that I understand your true reason for visiting the cell as...a bolthole...or as you put it, a haven, I feel that it is safe to explain the situation. Please understand that if Useful was to find out – following the enormous patience and fortitude that he demonstrated whilst working on the lock – that, all the time, the door had been unlocked, it would embarrass him dreadfully and do his brittle self-esteem no good whatsoever. A slave's lot must be difficult enough as it is, and he conducts himself so well – displaying, as he does, such great ambition and self-belief. I

166

only hope that his menial station in life as a slave does not, in time, break his gifted spirit of optimism."

"I am sure," said Rudi, "that care and guidance from Paul is proving to be the best possible propagator for that fine young seedling."

"Yes, Rudi," agreed Plum, "Paul plants a seed and once planted it, invariably, blossoms into something indescribably beautiful."

CHAPTER NINE

Bread and Circuses – The Positive View

A ruler shall appear, one of themselves
a governor shall arise from their own number.
Jeremiah 30:21,22

On their return from the amphitheatre, the troupe flooded through the cell door amidst the clamour of their own excited chatter. Paul sat down in his chair and called for calm.

"Please! Can we all stop talking at once? I cannot hear myself think. Let us calmly, and in an orderly fashion, discuss our recent experience – Plum, what did you conclude?"

"Well, in my estimation, the show went extremely well without a doubt and I was more than relieved at the paucity of large feline fauna. Our audience laughed in all the right places…well, almost…and displayed sincerity in the emotionally touching sequences – particularly during the singing of the hymns."

"I must admit," interjected Paul, "that I was apprehensive about the hymns, fearing that the authorities might take exception to their overtly Christian sentiment."

"It is my surmise," said Epaphras, "that the melodies and beautiful singing touched their hearts in such a way as to render the hymns irresistible, in their entirety."

"And what about me and Rudi?" piped Useful, "They absolutely loved us."

"That success" suggested Epaphras, "could have been because, although the audience did not entirely understand everything that was being sung, they were completely disarmed and won over by your physical clowning with Rudi – which, I must say, was exceptionally good."

"Thanks, Epaphras," said Useful, overcome to the verge of embarrassment.

"And what about the play?" enquired Luke. "That seemed to go well…but not in the way I expected. As Plum said, they laughed in all the right places, but in my estimation, it was the play that proved the exception. They did not seem to appreciate the humour but followed the story intently as if it were a legitimate drama and not, as intended, a comedy."

"Maybe," ventured Plum, "the fault for that lies with me. I went out, as you will remember, to address the audience beforehand, to explain the original play, Hamlet – particularly its proliferation of soliloquies from the main protagonist and how those soliloquies provided rich material just begging to be lampooned. Maybe I just did not explain clearly enough, or it is possible that humour relies on the culture in which it is created? I know that with passing time, humour can become dated… what is found to be funny today might not prove so to ensuing generations; unless the humour is classic, which can remain risible, seemingly, forever. But only passing time can decide that."

"We found it funny, as did the governor," said Paul.

"Then there is no accounting for the audience's reaction," said Plum.

"Maybe they saw King Claudius as a Roman Emperor and were watching in fear and trepidation of what was to become of Hamlet, when he performed the forbidden play in front of him?"

"You may be right, but why worry, as they seem to thoroughly enjoy it anyway," commented Demas.

"I suppose you are right Demas - and what about the dancing? There was no equivocation there. I glanced up at the terraces and was surprised and delighted to see a swaying, shuffling mass of Roman citizenry tripping the light fantastic with complete abandon – joy unbounded."

"And what about the governor!" chirruped Useful.

"Ah! so *you* noticed too Useful?" said Paul, "For all the momentous sights and sounds of the event, my abiding memories will be of the governor. On arrival at the amphitheatre, there, as expected but dreaded, was Alexander the coppersmith with his gang of snarling savages – all out to ruin the day. But, on seeing the governor they, for some inexplicable reason, became cowed and bleated like sheep – in fact, like little lambs. The governor on his part said nothing, but, appeared to control them purely by his presence."

"And what a presence!" said Plum. "I do not know what it is about that man but he has a calming munificence, which is most uncanny. He is not your usual eviscerating, behave yourself or else, sledge hammer of a Roman prison governor; you know, the type that come in the large, economy size pack."

"Do you have the feeling that we are, for some obscure reason, being protected?"

"You mean for some greater purpose, Luke?" queried Paul. "We do have God's work to accomplish by establishing his kingdom here on earth."

"Protection provided by a prison governor?" queried Demas, "Hardly the quarter from which one might expect such a service."

"It reminds me of Daniel in the Den of Lions," said Aristarchus.

"Maybe, like Daniel, we were rescued because we trusted in our God?"

"But there were no lions to be rescued from," piped Useful.

"Well there could just as easily have been and maybe our rescuer prevented them," replied Aristarchus.

"For Daniel, God shut the mouths of lions…and for us he shut the mouths of Alexander the coppersmith and his crowing cronies", laughed Useful.

"Well, let us think ourselves fortunate that we were rescued and thank God for it," said Luke.

"Amen!" Came the unanimous reply.

As the echo of the cellmates' word of concurrence rattled around the room, the door was flung open and in walked, or should that be, *skipped*, Prisca, followed by two slaves carrying that, now familiar, stretcher or bier, on which were balanced those, also familiar, wooden containers. They were followed by Aquila and Rudi, who was dressed in what looked like the original coat of many colours, but with a few Rudi extras such as long flowing sleeves that widened considerably from the shoulder to the wrist, revealing his hands but with a pointy part which flowed down to the ground. Prisca, face aglow and beaming, cried, "Congratulations to you all! You were brilliant…and so professional. It was a performance that will be remembered in Rome and further a-field for generations!"

"Thank you for those kind words Prisca," said Paul, "They are most appreciated, and in the hope of not sounding too immodest, I think - and I am sure, so do the others - that we excelled ourselves. But heaven knows how we did it?"

"Oh," said Plum, "heaven probably knows perfectly well how we did it and is proud of its own involvement."

"Then," said Paul, "we must thank God for our success and for his boundless grace."

"Amen!" was once again the cry.

Thanks were also offered for the benevolence of Prisca and Aquila, followed by the biggest end-of-run (although a run of only one performance) party that the theatrical world has, probably, ever seen.

◆

Time passed and as the memories of the glorious day at the amphitheatre and the ensuing celebration faded, the atmosphere in the cell became very flat. There were no rehearsals to look forward to, which, in turn, led to an air of pointlessness - even the spontaneous hymn singing became difficult, as it reminded them of the lost excitement of the heady days of the build-up to the show. Of course, Plum was not flat of mood or down cast, as he had his novel to write, which he now did with great fervour. Paul had his churches to write to and administer, and his business correspondence to attend to and so had no time to allow inactivity to weigh him down, as it was doing with those around him.

"I'm bored," moaned a despondent Useful.

"Pardon?" said Plum, lifting his eyes from his typescript and looking quizzically at him.

"I'm bored, I'm *really* bored."

"A young laddie like you, bored? I can't understand it," said Plum. "Why when I was your age I could always find something to do."

"Were you in prison at the time, then?"

"No, of course not but with a young boy's imagination, the world was my oyster. I could be sailing the seven seas or..."

"But there aren't seven seas," interjected Paul.

Realising his time-enforced gaff, Plum blustered,

"Well, however many seas there are, I could be sailing them."

"Why?" queried Useful.

"Why?... Why?" retorted Plum, tempted to go for a third, 'Why,' à la Rudi. "I will, tell you why: because God has blessed me with the ability to imagine whatever situation I choose to place myself in; whether it be at the Olympic games, winning laurel wreaths galore for my magnificent feats of athleticism; escaping from locks and chains in a large tank of water, or...."

"Did you have to mentioned that," moaned Useful.

"Sorry, Useful, I did not mean to upset you."

"Remember Useful," interposed a grinning Demas, "*All experience is good experience.*"

"Anyway," continued Plum," I think you must understand

what I mean. Which is: if you have collected lots of ideas, thoughts, and images, you have enough material with which to create your own world and then retire into it whenever you need, or choose to do so. Believe me, such activity can save your life, or at least your sanity. I recommend that you try it sometime and reap the rewards."

"What would we do without mystery, imagination and myth, Plum?" said Paul; "It is a gift that separates us from the other living things on this earth."

"What do you mean by that?" queried Useful.

Plum obliged: "A cow, a dog or a sheep, or, for that matter, any other creature on this earth, to the best of our knowledge, does not know that it is going to die, but we know that *we* are."

"The fact that we are conscious of death," said Paul, "enables us to appreciate the significance of Christ sacrificing himself by dying on the cross and rising again; and his essential promise of everlasting life for those who wish to enter the kingdom by choosing Him as The Way."

"Then with such a promise we wait in joyful anticipation of that Kingdom and must leave no room in our minds for boredom," enjoined Luke.

"Good man!" exclaimed Paul, "Well said!"

"Talking of, mystery, imagination and myth," said Plum, "such facilities enable us to transcend the ordinary. It is as if one's mind is a room in which a door is found you thought was locked but manage to push open. Before you push it open you can conjecture as to what lies on the other side of it. The possibilities are infinite. It is similar to the topography of the earth – hills and mountains are there so that we are encouraged to indulge in the mystery of what lies beyond them."

"Those same facilities make it possible for us to hold in our mind a concept," suggested Paul.

"And perfect it," ventured Luke.

"It could just as easily be an evil concept, though," added Demas.

"Perfect evil?" queried Plum, "What a dreadful thought."

"But countered by the joy of perfect good," added a jubilant Paul.

"Yes," said Plum, "it would seem that our world – and probably the universe - is one of perfect symmetry. Everything has its opposite, including good - which is opposed by evil. Perhaps the power of the Kingdom through Christ is the opposite of the power of mankind with its barbarism and cruelty, typified by the Roman Empire?

"And it is our intention, through the grace of God, to see that Christ's power for good is maintained here on earth," asserted Luke.

"Amen." came, yet again, the fulsome cry.

"I'm sorry about me being bored," said an obviously remorseful Useful.

"Do not feel too badly about it, Useful." said Plum, "Boredom is common among people around your age, until they realise the riches that lie within their reach – whether real or imaginary – just preserve that wonderful gift of hope and optimism that you possess and you will be fine. Or, alternatively, set sail in your imagination to discover how many seas there really are, before reporting back the exact number to Paul."

The mood in the cell began to improve as the cellmates

pondered on what had been said about boredom and its possible cures. Their focus became directed to their Christian duties and, once again, they began to relish their prayers and hymn singing.

◆

Plum had taken advantage of the unlocked cell door and was sitting on the low wall in the yard when along came, not Rudi, as might be expected, but, the governor.

"Good day!" said the governor.

Oh dear, thought Plum, I'm in trouble now.

"Have no fear!" said the governor, sensing Plum's unease.

"I thought that you might not approve of my being outside the cell."

"I have known about your short respites from the cell since you took your first one."

"Did Rudi inform you?"

"No! Rudi did not inform me."

"Then how did you know?"

"I have a gift for knowing all. It is an essential in my position."

Plum decided that if the governor wished to think himself omniscient and talk in riddles, then that was quite all right with him, and anyway what was to be gained from rocking the boat.

"Lovely day." said Plum, resorting to small talk.

"It is indeed," replied the governor. "Come, walk with me for a while?"

And so, Plum and the governor set off on a stroll around the yard.

"What are the matters that you are debating between yourselves as you and Rudi take your seats on that convenient wall, here in the yard?"

"Oh, this and that, you know," said Plum, hesitantly, wondering where this line of questioning was leading.

"Did you know each other before you arrived here?"

"Oh, oh, thought Plum, it is the old third degree. He is interrogating me about my relationship with Rudi…he probably thinks that we are spies. An Englishman talking animatedly to a German soldier in broad daylight… how foolish we have been. But, wait a minute… he is supposed to be a Roman prison governor in the first century AD, why would such matters be of concern to him?

"No, we did not know each other before, we just became friends through his regular visits to the cell and our mutual interest in the theatre."

"I hear that you are a writer Plum – may I call you Plum?"

"Of course, you may…everybody does…except Rudi, that is. For some reason, he cannot bring himself to do so."

Plum was about to enquire about the governor's name but thought better of it. For some reason that he couldn't quite put his finger on, it somehow did not seem appropriate at that particular time.

"And that you write comedy," continued the governor.

"Yes, that is true." replied Plum, "Novels and lyrics for musical shows, mostly."

"Do you enjoy what you do?"

"Oh, immensely." replied Plum. "Mind you, some people find comedy a little lightweight; they consider that comedy cannot be taken seriously."

"I thought that that was the general idea," said the governor, chuckling.

"No, I mean, when compared with serious writings such as that of great poets. Say, for instance, people in your cultural history such as Catallus, Ovid or Virgil."

"Great men all!" exclaimed the governor enthusiastically "…beautifully written but with, at times, questionable content."

"And probably most, if not all of them, influenced and inspired by that great woman, Sappho," said Plum.

"I appreciate their work - all those you mention; but really you should not think yourself, or your work, as being less essential than theirs. You see, to me all great writers and performers belong to an invaluable body of what I call, *Joy Bringers*. They are blessed with the talent, and therefore the opportunity, to bring joy to mankind. That is why I admired and enjoyed your show…you were, and are, providing a vital service to people who are making their way through the trials of life. There are many obstacles to overcome and your comedy can make their heavy loads seem lighter."

"I never thought of it that way," said Plum, "In fairness, I too derive a great deal of joy from carrying out my work of comedy writing. I did not embark, as you imply, on a mission to cheer up my fellow man. It was just something that I felt compelled to do."

"Compelled? And by whom?"

"I do not know…it feels as though it was what I was born to do."

"Precisely!" said a smiling governor. "My point exactly. And think yourself very blessed indeed that you are a part of that precious body; you are a *Joy Bringer*."

"So," ventured Plum. "I am an altruist without knowing it"

"There is no such thing as altruism," said a smiling governor.

"Oh, surely there is." retorted Plum"…well… why would there be a word for it if it did not exist?"

"Some people set out to be altruists, but they always fail," said, a still smiling, but resolute governor.

"How can that be?"

"You must know yourself, from experience, that the more joy and happiness that you spread and the more kindness you extend to others, the greater the rewards – whether you set out to gain them or not. Love and kindness when dispensed, come flowing back to you several-fold. It is inescapable."

"Do you know?" said a now enlightened Plum, "Now that you have pointed it out, I have to agree that you are exactly right. Since my comedy writing career took off, my life has been one of great joy and happiness… although, I must also admit, my school days were pretty good too!"

"Well, here we are back at our perch – the heaven-sent low wall," proclaimed the governor. Do you have anything to eat?"

"I have no food to offer you, I am afraid," said Plum.

"Ah, but I have some that I must share with you."

The governor removed a bag that hung from his shoulder by a long strap, placed it on the ground by the wall and took from it some bread which he broke before giving a piece to Plum.

"That is most kind of you," said Plum, taking what seemed like, to a hungry prisoner, an unexpected bonus. Food was so scarce and difficult to come by that any small extra morsel is highly prized."

As they sat there in silence enjoying their impromptu repast,

Plum became suffused with joy – so much so that the thought crossed his mind that this is what some people would describe as ecstasy. There seemed to be no apparent reason as to why he should feel the way he did. There he was sitting in a prison yard with a Roman prison governor – an uncommonly kind prison governor, it must be said - chewing a scrap of bread and feeling as if all the mysteries of the universe were being revealed to him.

"Would you like some wine," the governor asked, handing him a goblet.

Plum took it with a nod and a smile of gratitude and began to sip it slowly, so as not to miss a single moment of the crowning bliss afforded by this extraordinary act.

Both having sat in complete peace for a while, the governor rose to his feet and said, "I must leave you now to carry on my work elsewhere. Thank you so much for your company and for the good works that you do. May your release from this place come soon and may you be delivered swiftly back into the bosom of your family."

Lost for words, Plum gazed up into the benevolent face of this exceptional man and bowed his head slightly, in respect.

◆

"What a day!" exclaimed Paul as he prepared his rudimentary bed on the hard, stone floor, "What an extraordinary day!"

"As some of my readers, on a far-flung continent, to the West, might say: 'You can say that again, buddy!'" Plum replied.

Paul continued: "Being escorted out to the amphitheatre by a cohort of centurions; seeing the coppersmiths mysteriously

181

brought to heel and then having to walk out into that vast arena to perform in front of an equally vast crowd; and all whilst wondering if we were going to be attacked by wild animals, is not good for the constitution."

"Not the kind of thing that might be prescribed for calming the nerves, Paul. It is like popping in to see the family doctor to explain that you have been feeling the strain lately and require a little salve of some sort to calm the nerves. Then the Doc. umms, ahhs and scratches his chin for a while, before scribbling and handing you an almost illegible slip of paper - which to make things worse is written in Latin. You get back home and go nearly boss-eyed attempting to decipher, in candlelight, mind you, its instructions. Which turn out to be:

a) Obtain a cohort of centurions.
b) Procure irate coppersmiths (around 12-14).
c) Locate large arena.
d) Check thoroughly for wild animals (preferably large and ferocious).
e) Appoint vast crowd of people (select carefully to ensure their love of blood sports).
f) Immerse yourself in all of the above, for about two hours.

Oh, thanks Doc! That is just what I needed."

"Plum, do you ever take anything seriously?"

"Don't be absurd, of course not. I fear that if I did so, I would go mad." And anyway, it's not my job to take things seriously. I spend most of my time keeping real life at bay - not only for myself but for my readers too. I find most of real life, as I am sure, do they, to be eminently avoidable."

"You cannot really mean that?"

"Ah but I do... look, the way I see it is this: as life is finite - beginning, as it does with birth and ending with death; between those two points lies the line along which your life travels from A to Z...or as you might have it, from Alpha to Omega. Now, as each day reaches its end, before it is gone forever, you can look back on it and say, 'For how much of that day was I happy?' It could be one percent through to one hundred percent. No matter what the amount was, it is now yours and cannot be taken away. It is in the bag, as it were. And so, if you can devise your life so that each day contains as much happiness and joy as you can possibly create, the grand total when you reach the end, in death, has been all yours and cannot then be taken away. You had it and...as I said, it is in the bag. Your life was as filled with as much happiness and joy as you could possibly have made it.

"There must be drawbacks to what seems to be such a dazzlingly simple plan?"

"Of course there are Paul. I am not promoting hedonism here. Your collecting and storing of joy and happiness must be done in such a manner that it does not harm or upset others."

"But what about the vicissitudes of existence? What about, for instance, when someone loses a loved one unexpectedly. You cannot then go around trying to make them laugh to relieve their pain of grief?"

"No, of course not, but you can offer them comfort through kindness, understanding and sympathy. You can do all within your power to lighten their load. I do not need to tell you, Paul, how joy can adumbrate in its many guises. Maybe, by the application of sincere care and sympathy, you can increase their own personal store of joy and happiness, thereby increasing their 'worst day' tally from zero to one – all those joy-points mount up to make that grand total at the end."

"You never cease in amazing me Plum. Your attitude to life and strategy for living it, in your particular way – and by that I do not mean selfishly – I find, quite refreshing. You seem to get along with everyone with whom you come into contact. How do you do it?"

"Well, Paul, it seems that I have been blessed with an ability to find things to like in the most unlikeable of people."

"And how does this blesséd ability of yours work?"

"As I have inferred, Paul, it comes naturally and so I do not have to make it work…it just happens."

"If you were to instruct someone on how to achieve what, to you, comes naturally, how might you go about it?"

"Well, I suppose it would mean going back to my percentages again Paul. I would tell them: after getting to know someone, evaluate him or her – not in an interrogatory way; nothing silly like that. Over a period, get the feel of what they're about and go from there."

"Go where?"

"Well, towards knowing how to value them and retain him or her as a friend."

"And how would they do that?"

"I would recommend that, in the absence of the natural gift that I seem to enjoy, they allot percentage points to them – not literally…don't write them down in a little book or anything. Just commit to memory how often they could be in that particular person's company before he, or she, becomes a little too irritating, might sour the atmosphere with their disturbing idiosyncrasies; or, dare I say, become just plain boring. Then, manage things so that they spend time in that person's company commensurate with the number of percentage points that they have allotted for them. That way, the relationship can be sustained positively and without having to betray its negative aspects. On family members and old friends, for whom one holds great affection, a hundred percent can be lavished – or more were it possible; and for those difficult people with whom we all rub shoulders as we make our way through life, just a few percentage points. But, each percentage point must come packed with sincere love, regard, and respect. Nobody gets left out and all are afforded dignity.

They will then remember their time in that person's company as one of mutual and relaxed happiness and respect. I hope that that does not sound too scheming or cynical. It really isn't you know, and both parties benefit. They can, of course, re-evaluate periodically to check if any of their relationships warrants an increase in percentage points – that way, steady progress can be made, by degrees, as it were."

"My dear Plum, you certainly seem to have human co-existence well organised, here on earth. I cannot wait to see your strategies when dealing with the hereafter."

"All in good time, Paul, all in good time."

CHAPTER TEN

Joyful Confusion,
Conditional Freedom and Shock

"**G**ood Morning! Herr Wodehouse."

"Ah Rudi, dear friend, how are you today?"

"I am fine, thank you…and you?"

"Although in good health…at least I think I am Rudi…well that is part of the problem; I seem to be in a state of confusion."

"And why is that, Herr Plum?"

"My life over the past months, since I came here has been a whirl of extraordinary sounds, images and experiences. Although, at the outset, I was resolved to just carry on as normal, I now seem to have lost my place in the scheme of things. I'm not sure if it is AD 60 or 1940. I'm not sure if my friends – including you – really exist or if I have had a mental breakdown and I am now living in a world that exists only in my fractured mind."

"If that were the case, Herr Wodehouse, do you think that you would be able to explain your condition to me so clearly?

The fact that you are aware of the reason for your confused state indicates to me that your mind is perfectly sound."

"So, what you are really saying, Rudi, is that it is perfectly normal for me to be surrounded by several people who existed two thousand years ago, and a character who exists only in a work of fiction?"

"Who's that Herr Plum?"

"You Rudi, YOU! You are supposed to be just a figment of Christopher Isherwood's imagination…Remember, I told you about his book, the Berlin Stories."

"Oh yes, Herr Wodehouse. How could I forget? He mentioned my Russian blouse…what was it he said about it… did he like it?"

"That is not at issue here Rudi; He made you up…*you* are a fictional character."

"No, I'm not Herr Wodehouse…I am here with you…in the flesh, as it were. And anyway, I met Chris in Berlin and I knew him."

"If you did, I doubt that the real character he based you upon, was called Rudi."

"In my guise as a…what is that lizard thing called?"

"A chameleon?"

"Yes, in my guise as a chameleon I have had many names and many identities."

"Oh! so it is just a rare coincidence then, you being called Rudi?"

"It is as good a name as any Herr Wodehouse and very common in Germany – it is a short version of Rudigar."

"Rudi, I should have realised that you, the man of many

disguises, could be relied upon to help clear up my confusion."

"Thank you, Herr Wodehouse."

"I was being sarcastic."

"What is sarcastic?"

"I think it must be an English thing, Rudi"

"Why is it that only now you are confused, when you have been here for months?"

"It was brought about by a recent experience that, as you might say, put the top hat on it?"

"Top hat? Do you need a top hat...I could lend you one – I have several."

"It is a figure of speech...I am sure that it is not your fault, Rudi, but a conversation with you can sometimes enter the realms of the surreal. What I meant was that it brought the whole matter to a head."

"Is that the head requiring a top hat?"

"Forget top hats Rudi. This has nothing to do with head-gear or any other item in your vast wardrobe. Just listen for a moment and you might understand what I'm trying to say. My recent experience occurred when I was sitting right here on this wall."

"What was it Herr Wodehouse...what happened?"

"The governor came by for a chat and a stroll."

"Oh, that was very kind of him. He appears to be a very sociable fellow."

"Uncannily sociable and, as you say, very kind. Why, in his position, is he so attentive and so...*good*?"

"Are you suspicious of him Herr Wodehouse...do you think he is...how would you say it...?"

"Up to something?"

"Yes, up to something. Something err…like your English kipper…"

"Fishy?"

"Yes, that is it, something fishy."

"That is my problem, Rudi, I just do not know. I cannot grasp what his motive might be."

"Is it necessary to have a motive for being kind and decent?"

"I would think it is if you are a prison governor during the time of the Roman Empire. At a time when everyone was under great pressure to conform, to toe the line…"

"Toe the line, vas ist?"

"Oh, let us not get side-tracked again, Rudi, I will explain that later. Where was I? O yes, what is his motive?"

"Maybe there isn't one."

"I am not usually suspicious; in fact, people say that I am too trusting - some go as far as to say that I am naïve in my trust - but in this instance, I cannot help but think there is something mysterious about his gentle manner…and his benevolence. When in his company, I feel different…it is hard to explain… elated…contented…gloriously happy."

"He has been generous with his time and support, Herr Wodehouse, but has he given you anything tangible."

"Ha! That is just it, Rudi, he has."

"What was that Plum?"

"First he handed me a piece of bread…then…a drink of wine."

"A bit if bread and a sip of wine? Herr Wodehouse, hardly the kind of bounty provided by Prisca and Aquila?"

"Ah but that is just it, Rudi. It has little to do with the quantity; it has more to do with what that morsel and sip provided."

"And what was that Herr Wodehouse?"

"Following my imbibing of the bread and wine, Rudi, I became suffused by a glorious feeling of well-being. I'm used to feeling fit and healthy but this was very different…this was in some definitive way…*significant*."

"Herr Wodehouse. Perhaps he is not the governor after all, but the prison Pastor and what he gave you was spiritual support?"

"Oh, Rudi, it was much more than that. I pride myself on being a wordsmith but I can find no words with which to explain what happened to me whilst in his company. The time in which we now find ourselves has a regime which does not accept Christianity and so they do not yet have Pastors – prison or otherwise. It is not in my usual character, but I cannot rid my mind of the effects of that experience."

◆

Sometime later, there was great excitement in the cell, as the guard (the one who looks like Rudi but dresses in clothes proper to the period of the Roman Empire), had visited the cell to inform Paul and his colleagues that they were due for release within the next few weeks. Useful was particularly elated and having difficulty with containing himself.

"Paul, where are we off to when they let us go? Are we going to visit the churches or shall we stay here in Rome…and, if so, who might we stay with?"

"Give me time to think, Useful," answered a concerned and, seemingly unsettled, Paul. "There are important considerations to be made."

"Like what? What's to be considered?"

"Oh, lots of things. Please, Useful give me a little time."

"Alright Paul whatever you say. And whatever you come up with will suit me fine, I'm sure."

Plum sat sullenly apart from the fervour caused by the news of the release of his cellmates. He was effected, as we are aware, by his mysterious experience with the governor, now compounded by the mixed feelings derived from the happiness for his cellmates at their release and the disappointment of losing their company and friendship.

Rudi entered, (now in his German uniform).

"Herr Wodehouse, I have good news for you. You, too, are to be released soon."

Plum had been made aware of this particular situation when first taken into custody. Among the people interned with him were some who were sixty years old and over and because of this, released immediately. It was considered that men over the age of sixty could not pose any threat as future combatants and Plum was about to have his sixtieth birthday.

Overhearing the news of Plum's impending release caused even more excitement among the cell populace.

"All we need now is Prisca, Aquila, a couple of slaves and a large box brimming with good things and we can start the celebrations," cried a jubilant Useful.

◆

The hubbub had abated and the cellmates were sitting or standing around and conversing in small huddles; Plum was, as usual, rattling away on the typewriter. Paul was sitting in deep thought from which he eventually emerged, turned on his chair, pulled it closer to his table, picked up his pen and began to write. First, he wrote the formal address to the person to whom he was writing (who in this instance was his dear friend Philemon, the owner of the slave boy, Onesimus - or as we have come to know him, 'Useful.' He then wrote a paragraph of thanksgiving and prayer before starting on the main subject of the letter, in which he wrote:

> Now, although in Christ I have no diffidence about telling you to do whatever is your duty, I am appealing to your love instead, reminding you that this is Paul writing, an old man now and, what is more, still a prisoner of Christ Jesus. I am appealing to you for a child of mine, whose father I became while wearing these chains: I mean Onesimus. He was of no use to you before, but he will be useful to you now, as he has been to me. I am sending him back to you, and with him – I could say – a part of my own self. I should have liked to keep him with me; he could have been a substitute for you, to help me while I am in the chains that the Good News has brought me. However, I did not want to do anything without your consent; it would have been forcing your act of kindness, which should be spontaneous. I know that you have been deprived of Onesimus for a time, but it was only so that you could have him back forever, not as a slave any more but something better than a slave, a dear brother; especially dear to me, but how much more

to you, as a blood-brother as well as a brother in the Lord.
So that if all that we have in common means anything to you,
welcome him as you would me; but if he has wronged you in any
way or owes you anything, then let me pay for it. I am writing
this in my own handwriting: I, Paul, shall pay it back – I will
not add any mention of your own debt to me, which is yourself.
Well then, brother, I am counting on you, in the Lord; put new
heart into me, in Christ. I am writing with complete confidence
in your compliance, sure that you will do even more than I ask.

Paul then concluded with a personal request from himself, followed by a greeting from Epaphras, after which were added those of Mark, Aristarchus, Demas and Luke.

As Paul put down his pen, the air was pierced by the high-pitched voice of Onesimus:

"Paul, I know, as Plum has reminded me, that what you write is very important; just for once, can't you put your work aside and enjoy the thought that we are soon to be free...think of the future adventures that we will have together? Take it easy for a while...heaven knows you have earned a break from your endless efforts."

Paul sat impassively and devoid of expression as he reflected upon what he had just written and the effect that it would have on the perennially blithesome young spirit that was the boy, Useful. Plum, from the prevailing atmosphere and Paul's recent period of silent estrangement, realised that there was something amiss. He decided that to relieve the tension - so palpably evident – that a diversionary tactic might be employed to improve the situation:

"I recently suggested to Useful that he go sailing sometime," Plum interjected, brightly, "and it reminded me of one of my sailing experiences. Did I ever tell you about a trip I took with my good friend, Guy Bolton?"

Useful interrupted excitedly, "If you want to know about sailing, you should talk to Paul – he's had plenty of experience… tell him Paul. Tell him about the times you were shipwrecked and the time when you had to take charge…how the captain deferred…is that the right word? 'Deferred?'"

"Yes, Useful," said Plum, "that is absolutely spot on."

Useful continued breathlessly, "And how the captain listened to you and saved…"

"I am so sorry, Useful," said Paul, "but at the moment, I have other things on my mind and so cannot do the story full justice…I will tell it later."

Plum resumed: "Anyway, we went along at the request of a very important impresario called Colonel W.E. Savage. He had suggested that his boat, the Dorinda, had proved a perfect place for conferences and so we were expecting that, during our luxury cruise on his large and expensive boat, he was going to discuss a show that he wanted us to write. It was to star a great comedy actor called, W.C. Fields and we were more that keen to be involved…"

Demas interrupted, "Oh, I see, Paul, that you are sending Useful back to his owner."

Demas was standing by Paul's writing table, holding in his hand the letter that Paul had recently completed.

"Demas!" bellowed an outraged Paul, "That is private corre-spondence and you should not…"

"Oh, I am sorry Paul, I just saw it lying there and happened to glance at its contents…"

"You had no right to do such a thing…how dare you…" hissed, a near apoplectic Paul, now so furious that he could no longer find words.

The damage was done. Useful, in shock, sat on the floor, staring into the void of the gloomy cell. Paul, bowed by the weight of sorrow and exhausted from anger, stumbled over to the boy.

"My dear, dear boy… Onesimus…Useful, I was going to tell you quietly and privately of my decision to send you back to your master at the earliest opportunity. The last thing I would wish is for you to have learned about it in this way. Please, please forgive me?"

"But Paul," said Useful, trying to be brave, struggling to stem the tears that now ran in rivulets down his young cheeks, "why would you send me away…I thought…"

"I know, I know, dear boy, it grieves me deeply, too, but believe me it is for the best."

"Paul," said Epaphras, "I do not want to alarm the boy further, but I am sure that he already fully understands that the punishment for a run-away slave can be death."

"I don't care," spat an angry Useful, "If Paul is sending me away from him then what does it matter if I die… I just don't care."

"Knowing your master, Philemon, as I do, you will not be killed, nor will a hair on you head be harmed."

"But I want to stay with you Paul. Being with you has been the only time in my life when I have been truly happy."

"And, so you shall be with Philemon."

"How do you know that? You can't be sure!"

"Oh, but I am…" Paul rounded on Demas: "Demas, seeing that you have had some recent practice, read to Useful the parts of my letter, concerning his safety?"

Demas hung his head silently before speaking. "I'm sorry Paul…I just…I just…I just cannot at the moment."

"Oh, give it to me," snapped Luke. "By your leave, Paul I will read it."

"Please do Luke as it is, obviously, no longer confidential."

Luke read through the letter speedily and in silence, before reading aloud the sections concerning Paul's father-like love for the boy and his request of Philemon: to have him back forever, not as a slave any more but something better than a slave, a dear brother.

Useful remained inconsolable.

"The reasons for my sending you back to your master are well founded and long considered, Useful," said Paul. "Whereas you will be free to go where you please, I am still to remain in custody but under house-arrest - most likely in chains - until I appear, as is my intention, before Caesar to plead my case."

Useful sat in silence, staring blankly into space.

Paul continued: "As you already know, Useful, Roman law requires the returning of a slave to his owner. For me to be harbouring a slave who has abandoned his master will undermine my case immediately…it is not only me on trial, but also the future of our mission to deliver the message of Christ Jesus of how he abolished death, and has proclaimed life and immortality for all who believe in him. Following my trial and, God willing, my acquittal, it is my intention to travel on to the far

West, to Spain, to preach the Good News to those yet to hear it. That journey will be long, arduous and fraught with danger."

"All the more I should be with you, Paul…I could be your protector."

"My dear, dear brave boy, your courage knows no bounds and it is that same indomitable courage that I wish you to apply in this situation. Trust, I implore you, in my relationship with your master. Be assured that as the good and kind man that he is, he will honour my appeal and welcome you back as a dear brother."

"But Paul, it seems like you're casting me away from you."

"I am casting you, not away but toward the care of someone who will now see you as a brother in the Lord. You are not the scamp who ran away from him but a new and special person, returning with an equally new purpose in life. One of certainty in belief, one with a focus and one charged with the spirit of Christ, whose work you will be aiding by returning to your master. You were naturally courageous before - you are super-naturally courageous now. Be at peace and trust in the Lord for he will save you."

"You make me sound very special, Paul."

"Ah, that is because you are very special, Useful."

"Then I will do as you say and trust in God."

"Not only courageous but wise…you possess exceptional qualities Useful and I am certain that you will achieve great things. Once we leave this place, it is my intention to request of our brother, and companion in the service of the Lord, Tychicus, that he travel back with you to the Lycos Valley and Colossae, where he can tell our faithful brothers the news about me.

Whilst doing so he will ensure that you, and my letter, are safely delivered into the care of your master."

◆

"Paul?"

"Yes, Plum."

"You were saying earlier that you are going under house-arrest after you leave here. Why is that?"

"I regret to say, Plum, that it is true. I have been informed that Alexander the coppersmith has brought a case against me with evidence with which he can do me a lot more harm."

"How did he come by such evidence?"

"I feel, Plum, that the fault lies, initially, with me. Epistolary correspondence is dangerous, as, under this regime, secrets are impossible to protect. I, as you know, commonly commit my thoughts to parchment in my many letters and it seems, regretfully, that Alexander has gained knowledge of a remark in which I refer to the Emperor Nero as an unrighteous man."

"Pretty serious stuff, Paul."

"Very serious indeed Plum."

"Do you know how Alexander came by this information?"

"It was in a letter I wrote to one of my closest friends and travelling companions, Timothy. Although I love him dearly, he is impetuous by nature and discretion is not one of his chief attributes. He probably said something to Alexander in haste, which exacerbated what is an already sorely inflamed situation"

"Do you have a defence?"

"It will be difficult Plum but on this occasion, I will have my dear friend and physician, Luke, to act as my advocate. He is a learned man and, together, we will do what we can to create a firm rebuttal."

"Then, Paul, my hopes and prayers will be for your safe deliverance from whatever might assail you during your forth-coming ordeal."

"Thank you and God bless you, Plum, I could not ask for more."

◆

The day came for release and with joy tinged with sadness, the cellmates gathered together and faced the door. Rudi made a dramatic show of placing the key in the lock, feigned difficulty in turning it before swinging wide the large, heavy door. Shield-ing their eyes from the brightness of the light as it flooded in, the gaol-worn, bedraggled troupe stepped out into the fresh air, which, after so very long in that windowless, dank cell was like taking a drink from a mountain stream. Paul clutched a frayed, cloth satchel in which he had packed his documents and from which, protruded several scrolls; Plum carried his small brown suitcase in one hand and his typewriter case in the other; Useful carried his only possession: his script for the play, and the rest of the cell companions carried the few odd items which, to them, were of value.

"Parting is such sweet sorrow," said Plum.

"Plum," retorted Paul, "you have a gift for encapsulating each situation with a precise phrase. How do you do it?"

"I suppose it is because I enjoy reading, and the phrase I

chose for this occasion is borrowed from the writings of our mutual friend, William Shakespeare – it was said by one star-struck lover to another, in one of his plays."

"Our relationship, most certainly, does not fit that description...star-struck lovers, indeed? Yet, the phrase remains precisely relevant. Your choice is perfect, as always Plum; for all of us, this parting, is, indubitably, 'such sweet sorrow.' And I find it hard to believe that we might not see each other again," said Paul.

"Of course we will." said Luke, "You will be under house arrest, which means that we will be able to visit you regularly and, anyway, I will be helping you prepare your case against Alexander the coppersmith."

"What about me?" said a distraught Useful, "I might not see you ever again...any of you."

"You will, Useful. I am certain that you and your master, Philemon, will come to visit me, here in Rome. Or, on my acquittal and release, I will come to visit you both at Colossae. And, by then, he will no longer be your master but simply your brother in Christ."

"So, you think that he will free me from slavery?"

"I am certain that he will."

"Really?"

"Really."

"Wow!"

"So," commented Paul, "I can look forward to seeing you all during my period of house arrest?"

"I wish that it could be so, Paul," said a disconsolate Plum, "but it is my intention to travel to where my wife is now residing, which is many miles away. I have missed her and our pet dogs, immeasurably."

"I understand Plum…but I too will miss you, as you say, immeasurably – as I am sure, will we all"

Everyone nodded or voiced their agreement.

"What about you Rudi?" Plum enquired. "What of your future?"

"Plum, Paul, Useful…all of you. I have a deep ache inside me caused by the thought of my loss at your going."

"You called me Plum."

"Yes Plum. Suddenly, I felt that I could. The warmth that you have all extended to me has, at last, melted away my difficulty with feeling equal to any one that I might encounter. You have proved that it is possible for me, and others like me, to take our legitimate place in society and to rub along with everyone else, without stigma. I dare not contemplate how empty my life will be without you all. But, I have to stay here to work – not for my government, of which I am ashamed, but for the governor, whom I have come to trust and is very dear to me. My period in your company has been, without exception, the most joyful time in my life and I thank you all for accepting me as one of your own. Thank you…all of you, for the respect that you have given me. You have shown me a glimpse of what is possible and given me great hope."

"Respect has to be earned, Rudi; and you have certainly earned that which we have shown you." said Paul.

Spontaneous applause broke out as everyone crowded around Rudi to embrace him or to shake his hand, vigorously. As they began to walk across the yard, it suddenly occurred to Plum that the last time he made this journey and left through the main gate, he found that he was on the streets of ancient Rome.

"Rudi!" he whispered, "how do I know that I will be back in Silesia, when I leave the premises, and not in ancient Rome?"

"Do not worry Plum, you will be where you want to be."

"How do youI know that?"

"The difference is, Plum, that the last time you were led to your destination, you were led by the governor. With the governor, everything becomes possible. If you follow him, your destination is safely assured."

"Then why is he not leading me now? To make sure I remain in Silesia, and not Ancient Rome?"

"Because, as you, again, take up the life that you were born into, it will be your will and not his that will determine your way."

"Which means that when he is not with me, I will always have to find my own way?"

"He will always be with you. All you have to do is ask him the way...after all...He is the way."

"Are you trying to tell me that the governor is...Jesus Christ...God?"

"No one can determine what you choose to believe, or what you choose not to believe. That is your choice."

"You really are a dark horse, Rudi...pretending that you were as puzzled as I was about the identity of the governor and all the time you were working closely with him. You appear to have already concluded that he is God. Whether he is Christ or not, I, myself am a Christian."

"And do you pray to God?"

"Yes."

"Then just keep the faith and press on. And give our love to your wife, your family…and your dogs, because that is where you are bound."

"If what you say is true and you are working for the governor, and if he is who we think he is, I suppose that makes you an angel."

"An angel? No one has called me that before… but I will tell you something, Plum…"

"What's that Rudi?"

"It is better than being called a fairy."

"Rudi, let us take wing!"

"Well, you can, Plum, but I need to remain here to assist the Governor…allow me to escort you to the gate."

CHAPTER ELEVEN

The Afterlife

Now that our once-fettered friends and their associates have left the cell and taken their rightful places in time and space, let us spend a little time reminding ourselves of what notable things they achieved during their lives and how, according to the information still available, those celebrated lives came to their ends.

Saul of Tarsus (Paul)

Following his two-year term under house arrest, where Paul was allowed visitors, to whom he continued to preach the Kingdom of God and the truth about the Lord Jesus Christ, his life is shrouded in mystery. Acts, in the New Testament of the bible, which was written by Luke (the same Luke who shared Paul's captivity in our story, and in reality) ends with Paul at his lodgings in Rome, making his declaration to the local Jews (Acts

28:23-28). There is no mention of Paul's trial or its outcome. Scholars and theologians have, over the ensuing centuries, given their opinion as to what might have occurred. It appears that he simply vanished. It would be easy to believe that, like Jesus, he became a victim of the casual brutality perpetrated regularly at that time by the authorities throughout the Roman Empire. Some declare that he was acquitted and made his planned journey to Spain, thereby completing his mission to preach the Good News from East to West of the then known world. Others believe that Paul became a martyr by being decapitated with a sword, as befitted a Roman citizen.

Strict and dispassionate historians conclude that there is simply no evidence to prove conclusively what became of him. What we can say for certain is that Paul's concept of Christ crucified and his subsequent resurrection, and it's meaning to the salvation of mankind, still resonates two thousand years on. Even if he did not make his journey to Spain, the work he had done up to the time of his possible death in Rome must, without doubt, be considered to have been resoundingly successful.

Pelham Grenville Wodehouse (Plum)

On leaving the ex-asylum at Tost, in Upper Silesia, Plum walked, almost immediately, into a catastrophic situation that was to effect his reputation and cause him a great deal of mental pain for the rest of his life. He stayed for a while at the Adlon hotel in Berlin, and whilst there, was asked by a German, Werner Plack, (whom he had met occasionally, before the war, at parties in Hollywood, USA) if he would like to broadcast to America, (which was still a neutral country at that date). Plack was already aware of Plum's likely amenability to such a suggestion, as he had been informed by Oberleutnant Buchelt, the Larger Führer at Tost, that he, himself, had asked Plum that same question and had received a positive reply. Whilst interned, Plum had received several letters from some of his loyal readers in the United States and saw the broadcasts as an opportunity to let them know that he was well and still writing. He recorded five humorous talks (meant by him for his readers in neutral America), which the Nazis broadcasted from Berlin: first to America and then, a month later, fatefully, to the United Kingdom.

Plum paid dearly for his innocent naïveté. Plack was in the Nazi Foreign Office and having an English writer of great repute talking about, as Plum put it at the time, 'Simply comic camp life in the lightest possible vein.' was pure gold for the German propaganda machine. Plum became a pariah in his own land as, William Connor (Pen name, 'Cassandra'), of the Daily Mirror accused him in a BBC broadcast, of 'selling his own country...for the price of a soft bed in a luxury hotel'; AA Milne (of Winnie The Pooh fame) accused Plum of dodging his duty in the first world war by living in America (Milne did not mention that Plum had visited the US in 1903, sold some of his writings for vastly more than he could obtain in Britain and, for the sake of his livelihood, moved to live there five years before the First World War had begun). Also, in 1917, when the United States entered the war, Plum had tried to enlist for military service for Britain but was rejected on medical grounds.

Though there were very many letters to the press and the BBC under the 'anti' category, there were also a number under the 'pro,' from such luminaries as novelist and writer, Dorothy L. Sayers, who wrote in Plum's defence, 'When he fell into enemy hands, English people had scarcely begun to realise the military and political importance of the German propaganda weapon.'

In answer to the recurring accusation that Plum had avoided military involvement in the First World War by moving to America, (he was officially too old for military service in the Second), Malcolm Muggeridge, British journalist, author and Satirist, related in his essay on the Wodehouse affair, that, 'in 1914, at the age of thirty-two, Wodehouse tried to enlist in the Royal Navy. But he was rejected because of poor eyesight.' We have already learned that he had tried again in 1917. Later, Plum and Ethel moved to Paris where, following that city's liberation, Muggeridge, in his rôle as a member of MI6 and attached to de Gaulle's services spéciaux, visited Plum at his hotel. There, he explained the seriousness of Plum's situation and the terrible penalties, should he be found guilty of the accusations against him. Having warmed to Plum's kindness and natural charm, Muggeridge became very helpful to Plum and his wife, Ethel, commenting later, that Wodehouse was, 'ill-fitted to live in an age of ideological conflict.'

Author, writer and journalist, George Orwell, wrote a stout defence for Plum in which he explained Plum's ignorance of world affairs and politics. He also picked up on the point made by Dorothy L. Sayers' concerning the change in the mind-set of the British public during Plum's period of incarceration. Here is a short excerpt from his essay, In Defence of P.G. Wodehouse:

The other thing one must remember is that Wodehouse happened to be taken prisoner at just the moment when the war reached its desperate phase. We forget these things now, but until that time feelings about the war had been noticeably tepid. There was hardly any fighting, the Chamberlain Government was unpopular, eminent publicists were hinting that we should make a compromise peace as quickly as possible, trade union and Labour Party branches all over the country were passing anti-war resolutions. Afterwards, of course, things changed. The Army with difficulty extricated from Dunkirk, France collapsed, Britain was alone, the bombs rained on London, Goebbels announced that Britain was to be "reduced to degradation and poverty." By the middle of 1941 the British people knew what they were up against and feelings against Germany were far fiercer than before. But Wodehouse had spent the intervening years in internment, and his captors seem to have treated him reasonably well. He had missed the turning-point of the war, and in 1941 he was still reacting in terms of 1939. He was not alone in this. On several occasions about this time the Germans brought captured British soldiers to the microphone, and some of them made remarks at least as tactless as Wodehouse's. They attracted no attention, however. And even outright quislings like John Amery was afterwards to arouse much less indignation than Wodehouse had done.

Some considerable time later, in 1975, when the bitter enmity of the war had abated sufficiently and Plum's wartime misdemeanour was generally acknowledged as being caused by nothing worse than foolishness, the award of a knighthood confirmed his official reconciliation with his home country. Six weeks later, on St Valentine's Day, at the age of ninety-three, he passed away peacefully in his armchair - his tobacco pouch in his hand and his latest manuscript lying nearby.

Besides reaping the rewards of his genius as a writer during his life, Plum also suffered enormous disappointment. In addition to the calamitous results of the broadcasts that he made from Germany, he also suffered, during his period of internment, the heartache caused by the tragic death of his beloved stepdaughter, Leonora. And so, after such ravages, whatever the state of his Christian faith toward the end of his life, there is no disputing the fact that Pelham Grenville Wodehouse was a product of Christendom.

Luke

Luke's extensive travels with Paul provided him with opportunities to interview many people whose experiences were to be included in his scholarly writings. As a chronicler of the rise of Christianity, his written works provided the principal source of what life was really like for the members of the earliest Christian communities. As mentioned earlier, he wrote "The Acts of the Apostles," which, for some mysterious reason, ended abruptly and without an explanation of what happened to Paul, following his trial in Rome. Three years previously, in around 60 AD and whilst Paul was in Prison at Caesarea, he had written a volume now known as 'The Gospel According to Saint Luke.'

Saint Luke's gospel is particularly interesting in that it is the only gospel to include the Christmas story (Luke 2: 1-20). It is even widely accepted that Luke's source for that wonderful tale was Mary, the mother of Jesus. He learned about and recorded other event, essential to the passing on of the details of the early life of Christ, such as: The Visitation (Luke1: 39-56) which became the prayer the Magnificat, and the Annunciation, where the virgin Mary was informed by the angel Gabriel that she was to give birth to Jesus (Luke 1: 26-38).

It is also interesting to note that in Luke's prologue to The Acts of the Apostles, he deals with the question of the time of Christ's return to restore the kingdom of heaven. Unlike Paul, who seemed certain that Christ would return in his (Paul's) lifetime, Luke reveals a different theology by returning to the last words of Christ, when Jesus was speaking to the apostles before his ascension to heaven:

'It is not for you to know times or dates that the Father has decided by his own authority but you will receive power when the Holy Spirit comes on you, and then you will be my witnesses not only in Jerusalem but throughout Judaea and Samaria, and indeed to the ends of the earth.' (Acts 1: 7-8)

Thus, Luke cooled overeager speculation within the church concerning the exact time at which the Saviour would return, and with him, the end of the age. During the interim, this has eased the church into its proper role of faithful mission.

Luke's death, as with that of Paul's is shrouded in controversy. One explanation given was that he was killed by an idolatrous Greek priest, who, supposedly, strangled him before hanging him by the neck from an olive tree; another has it that he died in Thebes. The original grave of Luke, the man named by Paul, his 'Beloved physician,' became the destination for many believers in their search for cures for their ailments and, it is reported, that miracles of healing occurred there. In 357, when Christians were no longer persecuted, Constantus, son of Constantine, issued an order that Luke's remains be transported to Constantinople. It is believed that they now lie beneath the altar in the Church of the Holy Apostles, together with the remains of disciples Andrew and Timothy. Luke is now known as the Patron Saint of Physicians, Artists, Brewers and Butchers.

Aristarchus

Aristarchus, a native of Thessalonica in Macedonia, proved to be a faithful companion to Paul, particularly after they were caught up in the debacle with the silversmiths at Ephesus and in danger of losing their lives (Acts19: 23-29). This, as mentioned by Paul in our story, took place before a similar situation that arose with the coppersmiths at Rome (2 Timothy 4:14). Aristarchus accompanied Paul on his journey to Rome (Acts 27:2), during which they became involved in a shipwreck (Acts 27:9-44). Eventually they landed in Rome, where he became Paul's fellow prisoner. To say that Aristarchus was a 'fellow sufferer' of Paul's would not be overstating the dedication shown by this brave soul, who's Christian faith must have resembled that of a band of steel. Tradition has it that Aristarchus was martyred during the Nero persecutions.

Epaphras

As Epaphras is mentioned only three times in the bible, little is known about him. In one of Paul's letters, (Colossians 3: Greetings and final wishes, 12-14) Paul, told the church members at Colossae, of how he (Epaphras) worked hard and never stopped battling for them. And, as a display of his affection for him, Paul referred to Epaphras, in correspondence, as a 'fellow labourer;' a 'servant' a 'faithful minister' and 'fellow prisoner.' It was in the Lycos Valley, in Western Asia Minor that, due to Epaphras' hard work, three Christian churches were founded: Colosae; Laodicea and Hierapalis. Because, Philemon, (Onesimus' owner), lived in Colosae, it was possibly Epaphras who brought the slave boy, Onesimus (Useful), to Paul.

Probably converted by Paul, in Ephesus, which is not far from Colosae, Epaphras visited Paul - originally, to consult with him on some theological difficulties that had arisen among his flock in the Colosaen church. He had prepared a report on the situation which he handed to Paul and which cheered Paul's heart. Paul obliged him by writing a letter to the church members (the Colossian Epistle), which Epaphras took back with him to Colosae.

Surprisingly, after leaving captivity with Paul, Epaphras did not, as might be expected, return to Colosae with Tychicus and Onesimus (Useful). Maybe he stayed with Paul in Rome. Maybe he returned to the Lycos valley after Paul was either released or executed, following his trial. Or, he might have been martyred along with Aristarchus, in the Nero persecutions. The truth is, we just don't know, as scripture does not provide the answer.

Demas

And what of that flawed soul, Demas? We have no further knowledge of him, except for a single remark made by Paul in a letter to his very dear friend Timothy (2 Timothy 4: 9-10), in which he says: "Demas has deserted me for love of his life and gone to Thessalonica." And, so it seems that Demas had succumbed to the attractions of the bright lights and city life. Very different from Paul, when exhorting the Christians in Rome (Romans 13: 11-14) to '...let us give up all the things we prefer to do undercover of the dark; let us arm ourselves and appear in the light. Thessalonica was, as it is today, (but now called Salonica), a magnificent harbour with an air of prosperity and commercial importance. Hardly the place in which to avoid the temptations and pleasures of the flesh and to, as Paul would teach, "Let your armour be the Lord Jesus Christ; forget about satisfying your bodies with all their cravings." Let us hope that, eventually, Demas remembered his Christian teachings and returned to faith. Such a return to faith would have taken enormous courage, as we now know from what happened to other Christians, under Nero, at that time.

Prisca (Priscilla) and Aquila

As they are always mentioned as a couple in the bible, we will keep them together here. As far as equality among the sexes is concerned: of the six times that they are mentioned in the bible, Aquila's name comes first three times and Prisca's three times. Aquila was a Jew, originally from the diaspora of northern Anatolia (now in Turkey), who believed in Jesus Christ and followed his teachings, and Prisca (a.k.a. Priscilla - a Roman diminutive of Prisca) was also probably a Jew, but, possibly, from Rome. As we learned from our story, Prisca and Aquila, like Paul, were in the business of tent making. Initially, they traded in Rome but according to the Roman historian, Suetonius: In 49, the Emperor Claudius expelled all Jews from Rome because, "they were rioting due to someone called Chrestus." (Chrestus...now who could that be?).

To escape persecution, Aquila and Prisca moved to Corinth in the early 50s and carried on their business from there. It was then that they met Paul and, subsequently, welcomed him into their home (Acts 18:3). It was in the homes of such people as Prisca and Aquila that the early Christian churches were established and where the local Christians read the Sacred Scriptures and celebrated the Eucharist. Eventually, they moved to Ephesus where, according to Luke (Acts 18:24-28), they were instrumental in completing the Christian formation of Apollos.

Apollos was an important Jewish-Christian evangelist in Ephesus. He was an eloquent man with a firm knowledge of the scriptures and a good grounding in the Way of the Lord Jesus Christ. It was whilst listening to the spiritually earnest preaching of Apollos that Aquila and Prisca realised that there was an important gap in his knowledge. Whereas he was perfect in the detail of what he taught about Jesus, he was only versed in the baptism of John, but not in that of Christ. They took an interest in him and gave him further instruction about the Way. Following that, he was able, in his energetic style, to demonstrate, comprehensively, to his future audiences, that Jesus is indeed, the Christ.

We know from Paul (Romans 16:3-5) that when writing to the Christians in Rome, he sends his greeting to Prisca and Aquila, which indicates that they had subsequently moved back to the Empire's capital and were, once again, using their home as a Christian church. In that same letter, Paul indicates his regard for the couple by referring to them as the ones, "...who risked death to save my life. I am not the only one to owe them a debt of gratitude, all the churches among the pagans do as well." Sadly, tradition has it that Prisca and Aquila perished as martyrs.

Onesimus

What of that bundle of vitality, the slave boy, Onesimus - or as Plum called him, Useful? (In fact, so did everyone else, as his Latin name translates as, 'Useful' or 'Profitable'). We must take it that, on receiving the heartfelt letter from Paul (the one that features in our story, pleading Useful's case as a reformed character and fellow Christian – and, in reality, carried by Tychicus and Onesimus to Colosae), Useful's master, Philemon, forgave the boy for running away and, it is thought, stealing some of his property. The only hint that we have of Useful's return to the right path and emancipation from slavery is that sometime later, an early Christian church father, Ignatius of Antioch, wrote of a Bishop of Ephesus called Onesimus (The dates are right, as that particular Bishop died in the year 95).

If true - that that bishop was the Onesimus (Useful) mentored by Paul - what a joyful thought: that that illiterate, streetwise kid with all his courage and aspirational drive, met Paul, learned about The Way from him, and was guided to channelling all his God-given gifts into the furtherance of the Christian cause. That would mean that Philemon had not only freed the boy from slavery, but had had him educated, helped him realise his potential and given him the ability to face the

216

world, not with street wisdom, but with profound wisdom. We have no information on how Useful died, but hope that he lived a long and productive life.

Rudigar Dressler

As the period was right and the character was right and as implied in our story, your author took the liberty of 'borrowing' this character from the excellent novel, The Berlin Stories, written by Christopher Isherwood. Although it would have been straightforward to create a new character to fulfil that role, your author could not resist the authenticity of a ready-made character with all the required period credentials. Created (probably from life) in the period of the rise of the Nazis, Rudi filled the bill perfectly. Owing to Rudi's love for dressing up, (re. His Russian blouse in the original novel and his dressing up box in our story) his second name, 'Dressler,' was added, in our story, for comic effect.

Some readers might find it difficult to condone Plum's warm relationship with a member of the German army of that period, but there are mitigating circumstances. In one of his camp diaries, Plum wrote, 'that Germans are swell guys, and the only barrier between us is one of language. I never met an English-speaking German I didn't like instantly.' It would, surely have been the same had he met anyone of whatever nationality. It was typical of his temperament that he would take such a view, but as to how he would react when dealing with his fellow man in the plural, as opposed to the singular, we don't know. He never gave his opinion on the German Nazi hierarchy but even had he done so, his naïveté coupled with his unworldliness, would make it difficult for him to be hostile - ill will did not come naturally to Plum.

Had Rudi, who in our story represents a persecuted minority, been found to be homosexual by the Nazi authorities, he would have been sent to a concentration camp to suffer torture or to be subjected to experimentation in a vain attempt to, as the Nazis thought, 'cure' homosexuality. The grim and dreaded concentration camp, Auschwitz, was barely thirty miles away from the ex-asylum at Tost, and Belsen only a half day's drive. So, Rudi, Paul and some of his colleagues, had they all been in Germany at that time, could have found themselves together in one of those dreadful places – two persecuted minorities: Jews and homosexuals. But in our story, they meet in an old 'asylum;' a word understood to mean either a place of refuge for people fearing for their safety or those fleeing the dangers of war; or, alternatively, a place where unfortunate people who have lost their ability to reason can be sheltered and cared for.

Though we question how Plum might react to people in the plural, it would appear that pluralism is instrumental in the creation of the circumstances in which the whole world becomes an asylum for the insane. One where the ability to reason is lost, where, initially, some unfortunate individual (probably psychologically damaged by a wretched childhood) seizes the opportunity to wreak vengeance upon the world for its treatment of him and goes on to convince millions that they too should exact revenge for their own grievances. Innocent individuals then become victimised and subjected to unbridled hate, and for no sensible reason. Why is it, as Plum and Paul agree in our story, that the majority of people are more readily motivated by being against something than for it? It is probably bound up with what they refer to, in our story, as 'Shakespearean foibles' (or one might also call, the unavoidable complication of the private agenda of the individual).

Cannot a species capable of landing men on the moon (and thereby changing, literally, the erstwhile, earthbound viewpoint of the whole of the human race) not use its vast intellectual ability to change the viewpoint of its own kind, to one of mutual empathy and positivity? But then again, not all we human beings possess towering intellects and would have to trust those who do ('Trust' now there's a word worthy of rediscovery). There has to be a way to overcome this occasional loss of reason – or will we have to carry on as slaves to our emotions, reacting, lazily, to baser instincts and disregarding reason and civility, simply because it makes us feel better for a fleeting moment. We are eminently capable of foreseeing the possible results of our folly, but persist in thoughtlessly tearing each other apart. Whether Paul's 2000 years ago, Plum's 1940… or our today: when the world has become an asylum is it not reasonable to plead for sanity?

The Governor

Who's the governor? The key to a possible answer, maybe? Then…that is your choice, entirely.

SELECT BIBLIOGRAPHY

The Jerusalem Bible, Popular Edition (1974)

Karen Armstrong, *St Paul the Misunderstood Apostle* (2015)

A.N. Wilson, *Paul the Mind of the Apostle* (1997)

Basil Mathews, *The Adventures of Paul* (1945)

John Dominic Crossan, *God and Empire*

Iain Sproat, *Wodehouse at War* (1981)

P.G. Wodehouse, *Wodehouse On Wodehouse (One volume containing three books – Bring on the Girls (with Guy Bolton), Performing Flea and Over Seventy* (1957)

P.G. Wodehouse *Money in the Bank* (1942)

Barry Phelps P.G. Wodehouse, *Man and Myth* (1992)

Robert McCrum Wodehouse, *A Life* (2004)

David A. Jasen, *The Theatre of P.G. Wodehouse* (1979)

The Illustrated Stratford Shakespeare (UK 1992)

W.S. Gilbert *Rosencrantz and Guildenstern*

Leo Tolstoy, *War and Peace* (Penguin 1969)

Christopher Isherwood, *The Berlin Stories* (1935)

Evelyn Waugh *Brideshead Revisited – The Sacred and Profane Memories of Captain Charles Ryder* (1945)

Hannah Arendt *The Human Condition* (1958)

The Times History of the World (New Edition 1999)

Rev. F.R. Montgomery Hitchcock D.D. *St. Paul's Second Imprisonment in Rome*